Ruin

Volume I

Ruin

Volume I

By Brandon L. Berryhill

with illustrations by Brandon Ellis
and editing by L. Farnsworth Colson

Authocracy^{Ltd}
Publishing

This trade paperback edition was published in the UK by Authocracy Ltd
40 Caversham Road, Reading RG1 7EB

Authocracy is a registered trademark in the UK and abroad.

The moral rights of the author have been asserted.

Series: Ruin

Sub-series: Ruin

Volume: 1

Trade Paperback ISBN: 978-1-914205-14-9

Printed in Great Britain and the United States by Mixam Inc

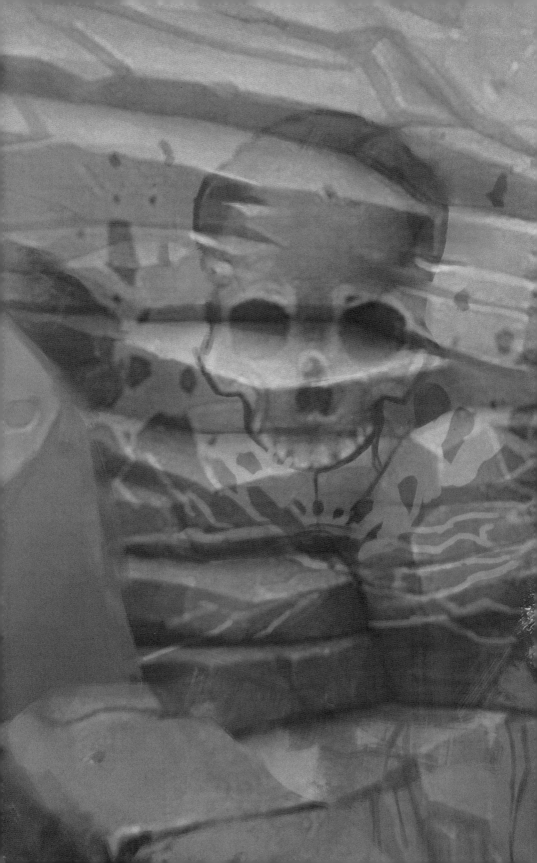

Prologue
Jim's Awakening

Jim peeked over the dune, careful to keep most of his body concealed behind the hot sandy ridge. The sun was starting to set, casting a brilliant cocktail of orange and rust-red hues upon the land, save for the tract which lay beneath the berth of his anchored landship below, its shadow gradually crawling eastwards.

He muttered sourly to himself. As he had suspected, there lay an overturned sloop in the distance, its tattered sail fluttering in the breeze. His eyes darted cautiously around the unmanned vessel. *It's probably a trap,* he thought, but the growls of his stomach protested against this assessment.

Four days prior, a starving suahim lizard had attacked him in his land cutter, nearly destroying his ship and what remained of his supplies.

The enormous creatures, sometimes up to three meters in length, typically avoided humans, instead preferring to feast on giant scarabs and other desert insects. However, when hungry enough, they could be a dangerous foe. Through the struggle, he'd managed to kill the beast, but not before it shredded his mainsail and snapped the mast in half. Since then, the wind had pushed his ship along on its lone jib sail at a limp as he pointed the bow in the direction of Freeport.

Drifting northward in his small land cutter, he had delicately sailed the rusty vehicle across the sands of the Great Dune Sea. With each new dune, he would dip, temporarily picking up speed, and then crawl up another. The Dunes offered little in the way of food or stops and it had already been days since a drop of water had touched his burning throat.

Smacking his cracked lips together, he crept along the perimeter of the rocks, looking for hidden threats. Jim's face was the only part of his body not covered by the heavy desert jubba, a loosely worn full body suit meant to protect its wearer against harsh desert sands. Scattered across the ashen surface of his garments, darkened spots of dried blood flaked off.

Pushing the lingering pain aside, he fixed his eyes on the downed vessel and turned an ear toward it. The sloop's sail continued to flap and the wind whistled through the wood railing. Jim sniffed the air, but he was upwind of the shipwreck, and the action was more out of habit than utility. Finally, he scurried his last few meters from the rocks to the steeply sloped deck.

The landship was similar in size to his own but in much better condition. He had to remind himself: food and drink before salvage.

As he shuffled quickly from the bow to stern, Jim made a hasty inspection of the small cabin through a broken window. The inside was empty, save a small bedroll of handspun desert cotton.

The creaking boat shifted in the sand as Jim made his way to the cabin door. Its port side pushstone lifted the ship at an odd angle, standing it slightly on its side railing before a new gust of wind brought it to the ground with a thump and a spray of sand.

In all ships, 'pushstones' were installed at forty-five degree angles within the hull to literally push the sand outward with their invisible force and prevent the ships from capsizing. Few things were powerful enough to knock a ship over in such a manner.

The fiery sun drifted into the haze of the western horizon, spreading upon the foothills.

It'll be dark soon. Gotta hurry, Jim reminded himself.

Carefully, he cracked the aged door to the cabin. Gravity did the rest. Free from the lock, the door flew open and broke off its hinges. It bounced across the tilted deck with a THUMP and fell flat onto the sand. Jim cringed. No explosions came though. He examined the frame. No wires; no booby traps. *Lucky,* he thought. *Let's see just how lucky…*

He forged on, careful to keep his footing on legs weak with hunger.

Crawling through the slanted room, Jim made his way to the bedroll. It was unimpressive and contained no hidden food caches. The room around him was a galley and crew quarters combined in one, common in small ships.

Jim rummaged through the cabinets but found nothing. No empty tins. No dehydrated fruits. Worst of all, no water. His belly protested in disappointment. Hope was giving way to despair.

Suddenly, a tingle began to crawl up his spine. A sense of danger as old as instinct. A growing feeling of doom was gathering in his gut. *Where is the captain of this vessel?* he wondered. It looked to be in fairly good shape. Little dust, nothing broken. Recently abandoned, he realized. Why would someone leave it here in the middle of nowhere, and where did they hope to go? The nearest city was days away by sail. Weeks on foot.

His eyes widened. *This is a trap.* In the desperation and mental fog of his full-bodied hunger, he had walked right into it.

His lower back muscles tightened and his hands shook as adrenaline shot through his system. His practiced calm was no match for millions of years of evolution. The animal part of his brain was shouting "danger!" and his body was responding.

Get out. NOW, his instincts warned. Outside, the wind had quieted. It was replaced with a *crunch crunch crunch* of footsteps on dirt. More footsteps, and then silence. A pair of bronzed legs came to a stop outside the crooked cabin glass.

With the dehydration setting in, Jim knew he had to act while he had at least some strength. He grabbed the bedroll and wrapped it around both arms. Shielding his head, he took few calming breaths before sprinting for the front window of the cabin. The thin glass shattered around him as he burst outside onto the still burning sand and barreled into the unseen threat.

The man stumbled backwards in surprise. Tossing off the bedroll and rolling to his left, Jim pulled a jagged hunting knife, still covered in dried suahim lizard blood from his last encounter. His offhand pulled a single shot pistol from a belt holster on his left hip. He was on his feet in a flash, moving quickly despite the nagging exhaustion.

A few paces away, an imposing man stumbled back, eyes wide, teeth bared. The hulking figure was adorned with armor fashioned from sun-bleached bones.

Oh gods, a cannibal. Probably an alpha.

The man was huge. Jim was of average height, but this man was at least a head above even the tallest Alliance soldier. The cannibal's body was built like a steam room boiler, but there was a hungry, hawkish look to him. There was little time to think.

The cannibal was nimble, especially given his size. Despite stumbling, he had remained upright and recovered his balance. With a frightening roar, he lurched toward Jim.

Leveling his pistol, Jim fired his single shot. *CRACK!* The gun kicked back, belching a cloud of black smoke. The musket ball found a gap between the rib armor and burst through the behemoth's chest with a sickening wet *thwap*.

With a crooked femur knife in hand, and apparently ignorant of his mortal wound, the cannibal threw his momentum into a final leap. Rolling to the right, Jim avoided the majority of his mass, instead sending his left foot sailing into the giant's chest, further traumatizing the bloodsoaked hole. Giant or not, a point blank shot through the heart was deadly, and quickly so.

The cannibal gurgled once and fell face first to the ground. A small cloud of dust shot out from under his crumpled body. Jim wasn't sure if he'd imagined it, but he could swear the ground shook a little with the impact.

Shouts and sounds of shuffling footsteps arose from behind the fallen sloop, robbing Jim of any hope of rest. The lack of water was sapping away his strength, threatening to push him to total exhaustion.

One, two, three, five bodies leapt over the overturned ship with predatory speed. These cannibals were smaller than the first. In fact, they were easily a few hands shorter than Jim. They looked a fair deal younger too; Most no more than teenagers.

Wearing little more than loin cloths, and painted head to toe in unfamiliar black and red patterns, they were gaunt with the same look of desperation he'd seen in the first. Maddening hunger was heavy on the face of each of them. And with their spears in-hand, tipped with black crystal, their glares were especially menacing.

They were in a fury. Their champion was dead, their trap had failed, and their dinner was escaping. With only a few dozen paces head-start, Jim sprinted for the edge of the sandstone outcropping back toward his anchored ship. The group gave chase, although a few stopped to feast on their comrade.

Waste not, I guess, Jim thought.

The first spear whistled by to his left, missing him by only a few inches. The next missile found flesh, cutting into his right calf and opening a gash. Mercifully, his body dulled the pain as he focused on escape.

Jim ran up the gangway and dove into the hold of his ship, rolling into a run. He crossed the small space as quickly as his legs would allow. Grabbing two pistols, he scurried to the starboard forward porthole. Shoving the first through the hole, he risked a single breath before squeezing the trigger.

The nearest cannibal doubled over a fresh stomach wound. His blood-curdling scream hastened his friends' run as they leapt past him. They did not show the same interest in eating their fallen comrade, instead shouting incoherent curses in their strange guttural language full of clucks and gargled words.

Tossing the smoking pistol behind him, Jim grabbed the second. Taking aim at the nearest cannibal who was now scrambling up the gangway, Jim shot again.

Click. Nothing.

Dammit, he thought with frustration.

Taking one last peek, he spotted four more of them scampering across the sand, only seconds behind the others. They too had no interest in eating their fallen friend, instead opting for the fresh meat of an outsider, now trapped in his rickety little boat.

Jim shuffled to the far end of the hold, hunched under the low ceiling, and pulled a worn canvas off of a nearby barrel. The torn fabric fell away and revealed a wooden barrel nearly as tall and twice as wide as Jim. On its front, in bold white, hand painted letters was written: *Go to Hell.* A small frayed wick hung from a pinhole in the top of the barrel.

With a thud, the first cannibal dropped through the entrance. Despite his hunger, this one moved slowly, eyes never leaving his prey. He'd witnessed the felling of his leader and knew to treat this quarry with more caution.

He crept across Jim's small cargo hold, eyes stealing a glance left and right, searching for dangers unseen. His breathing was heavy and his gaze fixed with hatred as he raised his spear to strike.

Withdrawing a small match and board from his belt pouch, Jim struck it. The small flame lit the hold in the dying light. Jim intended to make sure that the last thing the cannibal saw from behind his dirt blackened face was a feral grin and a lit fuse.

Jim rolled out a side escape hatch, specially prepared for a situation such as this one. He turned back to see the cannibal's eyes go wide with shock. The creature had just enough time to register what had happened and shout a word of alarm up to the others.

With only a few seconds on the fuse, Jim spent the last bit of strength he had remaining, his body still fighting him with each step. As he dove for a small indentation in the ground, the blast ignited.

One hundred and twenty pounds of packed black powder made for a spectacular explosion. Suddenly, the world was white, and a terrific sound shook his bones. For a moment, the noise and light was beyond his ability to fully comprehend. Everything seemed to move in slow motion, or at least that's how he would later recall it.

The blast thrust his body downward into the desert sand, cracking a few ribs in the process. Trying to control his ragdolled form, he tucked himself into a ball with hands behind his neck. Finally, rolling to a stop, ears ringing and vision blurred, Jim looked back.

The gunpowder had done its deadly work. Where a ship once floated, a smoking crater remained, littered with splinters of wood and mangled metal. Heavy clouds of black smoke drifted lazily into the sky as the remains of his life's possessions burned away before his eyes.

Somehow, luck had continued to accompany him. He was alive, aside from a few scrapes, a few broken ribs, the damage to his ship, and a slowly seeping spear wound.

When his hearing began to return, the sounds of crackling wood, howling twilight winds, and shouts reached him. From behind the growing wall of smoke, two specters lumbered toward him.

Against the burning firelight, the cannibals were horrific, nightmarish creatures. Covered head to toe in soot and hunched over, with spears held at the ready, they approached like wolves, moving in for the killing blow.

The wind wailed across sand and rock, buffeting Jim's back, staggering him. His legs shook and his eyes blinked slowly… so slowly. He tried to will himself to awareness, recognizing that he was falling into a waking sleep.

His energy was spent. He had no more tricks. No more strength but all the will in the world to survive. He shook violently, half from terror, and the rest from utter exhaustion. *This is it then,* he thought as anger replaced all traces of fear.

"Time to work for your supper, boys!" he growled through bared teeth.

Jim limped out of his landing spot. Wheezing and concussed, he calmed his heart and steadied his breathing.

Ahead of him, the end to a life spent in the wastes, of barely scraping by on the bottom rung of society. Filled with regret and anger over such an ending, he would give them something to remember him by.

Too close now, they could hold back no longer. The bloodthirsty scavengers charged at him. He mustered a hidden strength, surprising even himself as he shouted his last dying breath. It felt as if his very soul was being thrust open and poured upon them. The rage filled him. Then, it consumed him.

The howling wind crescendoed to a deafening roar.

Charging in utter desperation, he was upon them in an instant. What happened next, Jim would always recall as something between a dream and an out-of-body experience.

He saw the terror fill their eyes. He watched from above a familiar body — his body — as the wretched remnants of a man swung his arms and hit air. No, he wasn't swinging. He was wielding the earth itself. With each swing, giant pillars of sand erupted from the dune beneath him and tore the cannibal's flesh from their bodies. At each desperate shout, a mighty torrent of earth would rise and crash into them.

Jim knew that what he was watching made no sense, yet he was oddly unsurprised. He simply observed what was happening as he floated above his body.

The cannibals attempted to flee, but it was too late for them. The shifting sand soon ran red with their blood. In seconds, their screams ceased. Their skeletons were tossed across the bloodied landscape and landed in a heap of gore.

Still floating above his body, Jim's reasoning seemed to return. He thought for a moment and realized he knew what was happening. In a book, or perhaps an overheard conversation; he wasn't sure where he'd learned the phrase. *I'm an awakened!* he thought.

Suddenly, he was in his body again, and the world around him was darkening. The released power had quickly escaped his control, and now he watched, helpless as his awakening took its deadly course.

The rushing wind intensified and swirled into a terrible maelstrom. Lost now to the power swimming through him, he could only hope that he would survive the immense explosion of power.

An intensifying earthquake engulfed the remains of his vessel to the depths and turned the world around him a glowing ember red. Every nerve was on fire. Every inch of his body was in agony. The sky was filled with a deep roaring column of sand that spun around him.

The pain was simply unbearable. When the darkness came, he welcomed it.

Chapter I

Changing Scenery

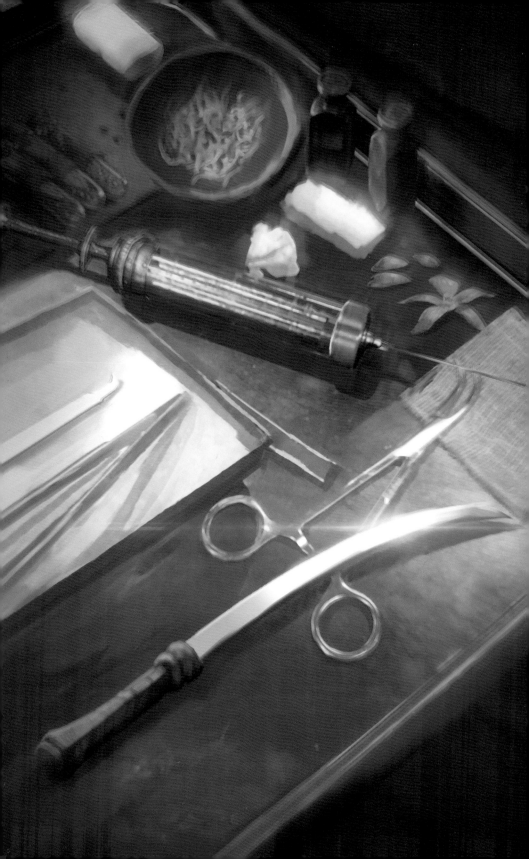

*T*hump thump thump.

A life spent between cities, floating above the sands had familiarized Jim with the sounds of nature. Wind, sand, scurrying creatures, and the slow creak of his landship as it lumbered across the Dune Sea. These were things he knew.

Thump thump thump.

The sounds of large machinery, by contrast, were an unwelcome intrusion upon a well established audible palette of familiarity. Jim's mind slowly sifted out the chaotic elements of his dreams from reality. Finally, blinking away a stubborn haze, he tried to make sense of the room taking form around him.

Walls covered with a patina of rust framed the small room. At the far end, an aged oblong door was fixed to the wall. The shining wheel handle was oddly matched to its dilapidated frame—like a bleached stone on brown sand.

Am I dead? Jim wondered as he studied his surroundings. A straight line was not to be seen. The ceiling, walls, floor, all of it was warped in some way, as if the structure of the room had been subjected to extreme force. That, or centuries of use.

Next to him, a flimsy steel rolling table covered with assorted medical instruments sat unattended. The scent of wood alcohol stung his nose before it was whisked away by a cool draft.

Among the medical tools on the dented surface, he spotted what appeared to be a large metal canteen. The sensation of thirst hit his stomach like a lead weight. Quickly, Jim grabbed the container and unscrewed the lid. It smelled stale and slightly metallic, but not pungent. Satisfied, he threw his head back for a long gulp.

Water slid down his gullet and was accompanied by a sudden wave of nausea. Jim felt as if his stomach had been empty for weeks. He coughed and cleared his throat before taking another swig.

As his focus and strength returned to him, he sat up from his bed., Which was cushioned and covered in faded tan linens. Taking a breath, he pivoted himself and swung his legs over the bedside. He set the canteen down and scanned the worn room.

All the questions of this unusual circumstance swam in his mind. *Where am I? How did I get here? Am I a captive? What did they do to me?*

A loud squeal and a metallic clang disturbed the quiet mechanical thrumming. Darting his head around quickly, Jim spotted a scalpel on the nearby tray. With sleight of hand, he retrieved the blade and slipped it underneath his pillow. Scrambling back into the bed, he sat against the metal grated headrail and focused a stoic gaze on the far wall.

The rusty door swung open. He caught a quick glimpse of a hallway lined with rusted metal and worn purple carpet runners.

Four armed men made their way through, lined up against the far wall, and turned to face him. Each stood at attention, or rather a poor mocked version of it. Jim stared at his captors. They all wore a brown uniform with red cloth bands on the right arm. He'd seen them plenty of times before. The armbands were typical Alliance Air Navy design.

The Warlord Alliance was the most belligerent empire in Ruin. The loose confederation of twelve desert warlords was held together by a burning hatred toward the Free Citizens Federation to their south, a people who had broken off from the Alliance over two hundred years prior and had been warring with them sporadically ever since.

When trading with Alliance cities, Jim did his best to stick to smaller settlements, the kind with few or no garrisons. Warlord soldiers were known for their cruelty and mistreatment of the lower class, and Jim was nearly as low as it got.

Anyone unfortunate enough to be caught alone in the desert by one of their patrols who was too poor to bribe them could anticipate a life of cruel slavery in the black-crystal mines, or, if they were lucky, a draft into the frontline death brigades manning the trenches. Neither was a very promising future.

This being said, something struck Jim as unusual about the soldiers standing across from him. All of them wore their uniforms poorly, and none were clean shaven, or clean at all for that matter. One was slightly overweight and the others seemed a hand too short. Even their breech rifles looked worn. One man was holding a muzzle-loading musket.

Once the soldiers had planted themselves against the far wall, an older man entered. His silver hair was matted with sweat and grease. He had a hawkish nose and small spectacles that seemed one small misstep from falling off his face completely. His hands rested steadily at his side and the smell of rubbing alcohol followed him in.

The woman who followed after him was
something else entirely.

She walked in the room with authority and
purpose. Coal black hair fell slightly over her
left eye, nearly hiding a thin scar. It ran the
course from above her left eyebrow down to
her jawline. The rest of her hair was done up in a
tight ponytail. Knee high mechanic's boots made
of leather and desert cotton met a pair of grey sport
pants covered in grease. Her button up shirt appeared to
be a few sizes too large for her and was so filthy that Jim
was unsure of its original color. *Almost white. Almost, not
quite,* he thought.

But the most uncanny feature was that she was present
at all. Women were hardly ever present in an Alliance
military unit, even as engineers. Warlords, and by extension,
their soldiers did not view women as peers—to the orthodoxy
of their society, women from Alliance nations were thought of
by men as only the means to the ends of homemaking while
they, the soldiers, marched off in the winter to make war.

As Jim watched her, he was suddenly drawn to her eyes. They
were the deepest green he had ever seen. Her gaze pierced through
him, and there was a powerful spark of intelligence behind those
pools of green. He found his practiced apathy falling away under
rising curiosity.

"Let's start with the easy stuff," the woman began. "What's your
name, and what's the last thing you remember?"

There was a moment of tense silence. Finally, a small grin
crept up the side of her mouth. She stole a glance at the elderly
man.

He didn't share her amusement and sighed loudly, "This isn't
an interrogation, son, and you may notice a lack of bonds.
You're not a prisoner here." The man's voice was still crisp and
powerful despite his age, "Ahh yes, you also may have noticed, you
are all patched up. You're welcome, by the way."

Against the far wall, the Alliance soldiers stared straight ahead, but
the tension was visible. If Jim tried something, despite their
appearance, he had no doubt he'd be on the losing side of an
engagement. He sat quietly for another moment, considering.

Finally, he opened his mouth to speak. The words came slowly at
first. It had been months since his last conversation with another
human being. Aside from the occasional swear word while
maintaining his ship, he was very out of practice.

His voice was a rough whisper. "My name is Jim, and... the last
thing I remember is... an explosion." It wasn't exactly a lie.

The doctor raised his eyebrow, "Jim? You look like an 'Izalatan; the forgotten class. I'll say, you're the first one I've met with a name like that. Don't you lot take pride in your traditional names?"

Literally translated, 'Izalatan means 'removed' in the old tongue. It was a name given to most lower class people within the Alliance as well as some traders, many of whom were descended from a culture conquered thousands of years before the first empire.

The 'Eternal Kingdom', as the first empire had called themselves, ruled the deserts of Ruin for nearly four hundred years and brought about many of the technological innovations that were still in common use.

"Doctor," the woman interrupted. "As you say, this is not an interrogation. Jim is a fine name. Welcome aboard, Jim."

Jim's eyes narrowed slightly as he tried to hide a look of confusion. The woman smirked and continued, "After we retrieved you, it didn't look very promising. You were charred, your head was a bloody mess, you had a good number of broken ribs and, well, at first glance, we assumed you were dead."

Jim's hands probed the bandages around his midsection and head. There was plenty of dried blood, but as he pressed on the various darker patches, nothing hurt or felt out of place.

He'd avoided the majority of the explosion, including the raging inferno. That much he remembered vividly. "Charred?" he asked.

He hiccupped as he finished the word, his voice rising to a squeak. He pressed his lips tight and quick, his eyes growing wide.

She smiled at his embarrassment, brushing her hair slightly further from her scar as she answered, "Both of your arms were completely blackened as well as a good portion of your torso. Over the last two days, you've been in that bed tossing and turning—"

"And healing at a phenomenal rate," the doctor interjected.

But healing like that... only happens when... a light went off in Jim's head. He'd heard of this sort of experience before. *I'm an Awakened?* he thought. The moments which had preceded his unconsciousness replayed in his mind.

Less than one tenth of one percent of the population was said to be a potential Awakened. "Natural" awakenings always followed a near death experience. The Awakened would often die from the release of massive energy as its previously hidden power erupted and often overwhelmed them. Very few like himself were known to exist outside of The Holy Land.

Those who did survive were hunted endlessly by agents of the Prophetess, the ruler of the Holy Land, said to be beautiful and deadly, and in possession of extraordinary awakened abilities. Those captured were taken away to be re-educated in the Golden Spire, the seat of government for her reclusive empire. There, they would serve out their lives as the Prophetess' devoted priests and priestesses.

The role of a priest was anything but peaceful and benign. Powerful as the Alliance and Free Citizens Federation were, they never refused a request for extradition of captured Awakened. Failure to do so would result in an army of priests "politely" asking a second time, usually making an example of those who refused them.

If these were Alliance military, it was only a matter of time before they brought him to the nearest monastery for a considerable reward. The Prophetess and her Holy Order paid handsomely for people like him. Awakened potentials were rare. Natural Awakened were almost unheard of and returned high bounties to their captors.

The doctor leaned in as the woman whispered something into his ear. He dismissed the soldiers with a nod, and the bumbling detail shuffled out of the room through the oval door. The doctor then made his way to the medical table and began collecting the instruments.

As the doctor organized his medical implements, the woman stepped forward and offered her hand. "I am Captain Alia Rychist," she said. "If you ever call me Alia though, I'm likely to send you back to this place with more than burns and dehydration. Captain or ma'am will do." She stared at him for a silent moment to accentuate her point.

Jim finally took her hand and shook it. He nodded for her to continue.

"I'm going to get right to the point, Jim." she said. "I know what you are and I know what they will do if they find out. Truth be told, I could make a small fortune for turning you in. And believe me, we could use the money."

There was another moment of unsure silence as she stared into him with her deep green eyes.

"However, that isn't our way," she said with a wry smile. "In fact, you should count yourself lucky to be here. We have a need for someone with your… unique gifts."

"I'm not interested," Jim replied.

"Fair enough," the captain replied with a shrug. "As I said before, you are no prisoner. Unfortunately, we aren't making port for some time, so I'll have to drop you off at the nearest dune. It should only be a few week's walk to Freeport."

Jim squinted and stared at the floor. Crossing the Great Dune Sea on anything other than a landship or heavily armed caravan was suicide. He gritted his teeth in frustration.

Finally, he sighed, "What's the job?"

The doctor broke in. "Before we continue, would you be so kind as to place my scalpel back on the tray? It seems to be missing."

Jim tilted his head sideways as if confused.

The old man smiled and added, "Son, if we wanted to harm you, believe me, we had ample opportunity to do so over the past two days." He and the captain shared an amused glance.

Jim turned the pillow over and removed the scalpel that he had carefully hidden away. He placed it hesitantly back on the tray, letting it drop with a loud *clang*.

"Thanks for that, son. I can appreciate a person who's always prepared for the worst. I assume your survival instincts, or an overabundance of luck, is what has gotten you this far in the first place. On this ship though, I wouldn't recommend running around and cutting up our crewmen. The captain can have awful bouts of meanness and, well frankly, downright temper t-"

"That's enough out of you, old man." Alia interrupted. "Jim and I have things to discuss, and he hasn't seen the ship."

"Ship?" Jim asked.

"He's a chatty one, Alia," the old man said. With a curt nod, he gingerly grabbed his cart and rolled it out of the room. The metal tray bounced and banged as he navigated the bowing wood floor out of the room.

"I thought you preferred 'captain'," Jim said.

"Benjamin's a special case. He's earned the right," she replied with a shrug. "Well, do you feel strong enough to take a walk?"

"Yes," Jim replied. His head was throbbing, but he stood, doing his best to ignore it. He swayed for a moment. The captain reached out to steady him, but he pushed her hand away. "I can walk," he insisted. Jim lumbered toward the exit, happy to escape his coffin. Through the door, the sound of the *thump thump thump* grew louder.

Most landships were purely propelled by sail. Steam engines were expensive to build and complicated to maintain, not to mention how sand and machinery are notoriously poor bedfellows. Only the largest and most formidable landships, usually within empire militaries, had the need and budget for such technology.

He couldn't seem to steady himself. Spotting his struggle, the captain said, "Don't feel bad. It takes most people a few days to get used to the rocking. I just hope you don't have a fear of heights."

"Heights?" he asked, confused. How big is this ship? he wondered.

Alia smiled mischievously and asked, "Do you know where we are right now, Jim?"

He recalled the details of his journey north. "I was about one hundred and seventy kilometers northwest of Vigilance Oasis." The words still came slow as he said more than he had in months. "If you've turned with the wind, that would put us umm..." His head was still aching.

Seeing his struggle, the captain added, "Somewhere a few days east of Freeport."

"Yeah," he replied as he braced himself against the wall, fighting off another spell of dizziness.

"Pretty good speed for a landship, especially one as big as ours," she said. They reached another hatch door. A tiny porthole spilled light into the darkened hallway. It was daytime. After being stuck indoors for days, though most of it had been spent unconscious, the sun felt warm and inviting on his skin.

"Thing is, Jim, we're not on a landship," Alia continued. The door swung outward, and a gust of ice cold air rushed past him. For a moment, he nearly lost his footing again as bright light blinded him and a gust pushed him back on his heels.

"And I meant what I said about that fear of heights thing," she gleamed.

Jim shielded his eyes and followed the captain carefully through the door on unsure feet. What he saw next would be etched into his memory forever.

Beneath him, he felt the familiar motion of wooden deck planks. However, these were thicker and sturdier than the ones in the infirmary. Still, they creaked with every step.

Grabbing hold of the railing, his eyes adjusted while he took in his surroundings. His hands gripped tighter as he drank in the scene.

Their ship was sailing through a sea of white clouds, their tops passing lazily by, nearly spilling upon the deck. From the northeast, the high Eternal Mountains shot up through the endless white blanket. Some still sparkled with the last of last winter's meager snow.

South, through a break in the clouds, The Great Dune Sea stretched far beyond his sight. The blacks and browns of each hill connected together in an endless tapestry of ripples and snaking ridge lines.

Jim leaned over the railing and spotted white sails and a glint of metal on what looked like a Brigantine class landship far below them. This far north, it probably belonged to the Unaligned League Ground Navy, patrolling out of Freeport. At this distance though, it was hard to tell. It moved along gracefully as its lengthening shadow stretched eastward in the warm afternoon light.

Pulling himself away from the breathtaking scene below, Jim began to realize just how big the ship — the airship — was. Above him, an enormous balloon of oiled, patchwork canvas stretched to the fore and aft of the ship. Countless small steel cables held it in place like a giant creature caught in a trap, locked in a hopeless upwards struggle for freedom.

Rope ladders wrapped the giant balloon every couple dozen paces and followed the canvas up and around the balloon, beyond his view. They creaked with each gentle push of wind, tensing and then relaxing as the ship moved gracefully through the sky.

The deck was crawling with men and women of every size and color. All were wearing thick flight jackets with the collars pulled up around their necks and faces. Just like the underdressed Alliance soldiers he had seen earlier, their uniforms were in poor condition. Among them, a few even donned thick leather aviator caps common to most empire military pilots.

A man, as wide as he was short, bent over a steel cable anchor with a welding torch. As he manipulated the tool, his exposed forearms twitched and tensed. A rubber gas tube fed the blowtorch. It coiled and snaked around the many obstacles scattered around the topdeck before disappearing somewhere below. Pieces of frayed black tape, hastily wrapped around leaks in the line seemed to be everywhere.

The man turned to glance at Jim and the captain. Captain Alia motioned for him to come over.

As he made his way to them he shot a calloused, soot-covered hand toward Jim, who needed a moment to pull his gaze from the bustle of ship activities. The man's vice-like grip certainly did the trick though. Jim barely contained a grunt as he shook the human equivalent of a pneumatic press.

The short man was all business as he spoke, "Name's Harol, lead deckhand. Pleasure. See ya around, then."

Harol pulled a pair of fogged brass-rim goggles over his eyes. He adjusted something on the sides and suddenly two dark lenses dropped into place. Harol quickly returned to his welding. He paused only momentarily to bark orders at a duo of young twins loitering nearby. The boys, teenagers Jim suspected, scurried off to carry out the man's wishes.

"Forgive Harol. He's a man of few words and many talents," the captain said. "Much like yourself, I imagine." She motioned for them to continue their tour.

Though Jim could not seem to figure out his balance, he did his best to concentrate and quickly shuffled forward to catch up to her.

From somewhere underneath them, the smell of burning coal crept up through slats in the wood and mixed with the sulphuric smell of black powder. The deck continued ahead for at least eighty meters.

There were two dozen eighteen pound cannons to starboard and what looked like a few thirty-six pounder downward-facing siege cannons above the forward quarter. All showed signs of recent use, their muzzles blackened under a layer of spent gunpowder. Crew members darted about, performing maintenance tasks on the carriages and structures holding the cannons in place.

Over the side of their ship, a pair of particularly brave carpenters sat on wooden planks suspended over the side by a few frayed ropes. They banged away with their steel hammers, patching what appeared to be a section of missing wooden hull. The hole was splayed inward as if something had struck and penetrated. They joked quietly and laughed, unphased by the thousands of meters of open air beneath them. Like Harol, each wore a pair of brass goggles, though these didn't appear to hold the same tinted drop lenses.

A breeze gently pushed against the side of the ship and sent Jim into the rail. He struggled to stop his vision from swimming. A strong hand from the captain quickly grabbed his arm as she said, "Easy there. You aren't going to puke, are you? We just repainted the hull at our last port of call, and I don't think Asad and Allie would be very happy." She nodded toward the carpenters as they waved up toward her.

Jim closed his eyes and collected himself for a moment.

"I'm fine," he lied. "It's just a headache." He ran his hand along the smooth railing, "What is this ship? This has to be at least a... Sunder Class Airship? What military do you report to? FCF? Protectorate? Alliance?"

The captain chuckled, "I'm glad you're feeling a bit more talkative. And no, we aren't Alliance, or FCF, or any empire military for that matter. As for the class, he's called a Dagger Class Attack Ship. It falls somewhere between a cruiser and a small battleship. Bit bigger than a Sunder."

"He?"

She sighed and rolled her eyes, "The male fascination with classifying ships in the feminine is so typical. You know, if most of my crewman thought they could get away with it, they would mutiny on that one little detail alone."

Another grin crossed her face. Jim found himself smiling back in amusement, though he wasn't "in" on the joke. Realizing how foolish he must look, he cleared his throat and returned to gazing about the ship.

Another gust of wind hit the ship, causing it to sway and groan. The captain seemed unphased as she stood and pointed at Jim. "You can have your lady ships, but this ship... oh no, he's no lady. He's a brute and would never be found in polite company. Though he is a survivor... and deadly when threatened."

Looking back to him, she smiled again. He noticed that the unscarred side of her lips seemed to rise slightly higher than the other. "I'm sure you can appreciate that."

She carried a confidence that he'd never seen in anyone, man or woman. Everything she said and did seemed to be completely prepared for and purposeful. It left him feeling somewhat foolish and out of place.

She had either not noticed him staring or had chosen to ignore it. Stepping over a coil of rope without looking down, she said, "As to the nature of our procurement of this lovely gem, that is a conversation for another day. Now, let's have a little talk about this newfound gift of yours and how it can benefit us both. You like money, right?"

Chapter II
Clockwork

Jim's tour continued across the deck to a door under the forecastle. The captain opened the hatch and stepped through, gesturing for him to follow. Ducking in behind her, he was surprised to discover he'd stepped into what he could only assume were the captain's quarters.

On landships, the captain was usually tucked safely at the back of the ship, but it seemed the sky was home to a different set of rules. Her quarters were planted right in the bow of the impressive vessel. The room slanted inward, the glass windows pinching off against a wooden beam that ran downward in the same place that one would expect a waterborne ship's stem to be. Replacing the bow planks with windows offered a breathtaking view of the world beyond.

The transparent panes ran the length of the room, disappearing into the floor behind the captain's bed. He imagined that, with the curtains up, sleeping in the bed would feel more like floating unencumbered through the heavens.

His eyes were wide as he watched the world from an angle entirely alien to him. The ship was sailing upon the wisps like the water ships of the Great Green Lake. In the distance, the Eternal Mountains marked the northern border of Ruin and the farthest he had ever travelled. He wondered at all the exotic places the captain and her crew must have seen. With an airship, they could go so many places that he could not.

Ruin was surrounded with natural barriers. To the north lie mountains, and the dragons rumored to live there. To the west and east, tremendous unceasing storms would strip the flesh from anyone who dared to traverse the deep desert.

For the few fortunate enough to survive, they could look forward to a swift and gruesome death in the jaws of any number of gigantic desert predators including the famed Sheraa dune crawlers. To the south, assuming you could pass through The Holy Land without drawing the Prophetess' ire, the corrosive dead sea and its toxic fog would make quick work of man and metal alike. The yellowish clouds extended far into the sky, preventing air and land vessels from passage.

There was a loud squealing and a clang as the captain shut the door behind him. Pulling his eyes from the scene outside, Jim watched as she crossed the room to an antiquated wooden desk gathering dust in the corner. A dried inkwell and neglected quill sat to the right side of the work area.

Captain Rychist sat in a creaking chair that fit in with the rest of the aged decor. Purple velvet wrapped tightly onto ancient Manzawood, fraying in some places.

In the wastes of Ruin, the Manzatree, more bush than actual tree, was the primary source of wood. The refining process from live shrub to manufacturable wood pulp was both complicated and highly lucrative. Due to the highly flammable nature of an unprocessed manzatree, it was also a very dangerous profession. Whoever had decorated this place, Jim decided, was fond of risk and flush with currency.

As the captain leaned forward with fingers locked, her chair creaked loudly, drawing Jim's wandering gaze. "Please, grab a seat from the closet." She nodded to his left.

Jim turned the worn handle on a nearby closet, withdrew a wooden folding chair, and sat down. A fresh wave of dizziness washed over him followed by a strong desire to sleep. He suppressed a yawn.

Seeing the weariness in his eyes, the captain asked, smiling, "Care for a cup of coffee? Our last err… procurement found us in the possession of over three hundred pounds of it."

Coffee, the sweet nectar of life; Jim hadn't partaken in years. The only place wet enough to grow it was far north of the desert, deep in the territory of the Northern Tribes, a hearty but fiercely guarded people who lived north of the fortress city of Stronghold.

Coffee was rare enough to stay out of the hands of commoners, and the southern empires liked it that way. Nobles were willing to pay handsomely for the heavenly black elixir. #

He couldn't refuse. There was no telling when, or if, the opportunity would ever arise again.

Jim nodded briskly, trying to hide his excitement. His groaning stomach immediately betrayed him. The captain couldn't quite suppress a smirk at his embarrassment.

She turned a crank from somewhere behind her desk, and a brass voicepipe suddenly emerged from a small pocket in the wall. She cleared her voice and called down into the pipe, "Henry, please make your way up here with two coffees, black. Our guest is parched."

There was a faint metallic reply through the tube. Alia leaned in so she could hear. Seemingly satisfied, she nodded, turned the crank back and let loose another disarming smile. "Before we continue, I'm assuming you'd like a little history on who we are and how you got here."

All was quiet for a moment. Jim cleared his throat, realizing that she was waiting on him, and replied, "Yes, please."

"You are a man of few words," Alia remarked, "but, don't worry, I talk enough for ten, Henry for twenty."

"Sorry," Jim answered. "Me and people... well, not too many good ones in the wastes."

A frown flashed across the captain's face. "Believe me, I understand." There was more awkward silence. Jim's stomach groaned again.

"Where is that damn coffee?" Captain Rychist wondered aloud. "Anyhow, first things first. You're on an airship. I hope that much is obvious now," she said as she gestured to the cloud blanket that drifted outside the windows. The side of her mouth crept up again. As it did, she brushed a few strands of hair across the scar on her face. Jim nodded for her to continue, trying his best not to study the old wound.

"As I mentioned, he's a Dagger Class Attack Ship with a few clever upgrades that, I'm quite proud to say, I helped install personally. This ship is coming up on its three hundred year anniversary."

Jim blinked. "Three hundred?"

"Correct. I'm this ship's fourteenth captain, matter of fact. He was launched from the city of Solitude back during the second crusade. I'm told he participated in dozens of engagements against the Prophetess' forces and was one of the few ships to come out of the war still operational."

Alia sighed and stared into no place in particular, saddened. "After the Alliance surrendered and turned its attention back to trench warfare against the Federation, he served the next two hundred and fifty years in boring peacetime roles. Poor baby," she said, patting the bulkhead behind her, "You were meant for greater things. At least you weren't refitted into a cruise ship like most of the big ones."

Turning back to Jim, she continued, "Anyhow, forty-three...four? years ago, it was...uh...taken out of mothballs where we came into possession of it. Technically, I'm his second captain, if you start counting from there. We named him The Liberator. Not a very creative name I know, but after all these years it's stuck."

Jim interrupted, "So... it... I uhh mean he, flew for the Alliance, fought for them, your crew wears Alliance uniforms, and you...aren't Alliance? Who do you report to then?"

Captain Rychist shrugged, "We don't."

"You don't? Don't what?"

"Report to a military."

Jim furrowed his eyebrows in confusion.

"Well, Jim, some call us pirates. Others call us rebels. I prefer to call us liberators. Hence, the name of the ship. You see, we liberate the undeserving of their possessions and put them to much more appreciated use. Our Alliance uniforms and cold weather gear for instance. Oh, and from time to time, we may liberate a monastery of brainwashed acolytes and offer them better lives."

Monasteries were mockingly called "brainwash schools," only in private conversation, of course. The splendent structures could be found in nearly every southern town and city, serving as a dark reminder of the Prophetess' victory over the Alliance and Federation hundreds of years before. When an Awakened was discovered, they would be whisked away by her priests, locked away for years and re-educated to serve her will.

"Awakened?" Jim asked, surprised. "You've actually stolen-"

"Liberated," she corrected him.

"Right, liberated Awakened from the Prophetess? How many of your crew are st— err, liberated Awakened?"

"All of them, naturally. Well, all but one, Henry, who is taking his time with that coffee, much to my annoyance." She crossed her arms and leaned back in the creaking chair.

Jim shook his head, "Sorry but... all Awakened?"

"Except Henry," the captain corrected him.

"Right," Jim replied. "But, all Awakened are taken by the Prophetess' followers. I've heard of some escaping to the desert, where they died. How could-"

The captain wagged a finger at him, "For someone who could barely utter a few words just an hour ago, you sure have a lot of questions."

"I'm a uh… curious person," Jim replied.

She nodded, "Smart people ask questions. Dumb people simply accept answers. Oh, and to answer your question, yes, at one point or another, most of the people on this ship were slaves of the Holy Order or on the run. I did mention we call our ship The Liberator, didn't I?"

Jim nodded and replied, "Yeah, a few times. But how were you able to break the Prophetess' brainwashing of—"

His question was interrupted by a sharp knock at the door.

"Come in, Henry."

A human figure, with a large brass ball where his legs should have been, rolled into the room. The machine was made entirely of metal. His outer structure was a mix of sheet steel and brass. Inside his human-shaped body was a controlled chaos of moving gears and cogs. Each one turned at a different speed as if it had a mind of its own. Behind the tangle of moving machinery, somewhere deep within the human form, dim blue light backdropped its inner workings.

The ball upon which it balanced was inlaid with thousands of tiny symbols. He wasn't even sure they represented letters. Though he couldn't decipher them, Jim felt he had seen them before.

His wandering gaze stopped at the thing's eyes. White light shone through mechanical irises which narrowed as the machine stared back at him. Despite their artifice, he felt as if he could see a person… a soul behind them. A chill crawled up his spine.

The machine man rolled toward them with a full spread upon a polished platter including sugar and cream. The captain introduced him, "Jim, meet Henry, our ship's quartermaster among other things. He handles the flow of materials — food, weapons, comforts. Oh! And he makes a terrific cup of coffee."

Jim couldn't pull his gaze away, "Is it a he? Or rather, is he an uhh…?"

"HE is a man," the captain replied. "A clockwork man to be precise. Judging by your expression, I'd venture a guess that he's the first you've seen."

"I saw one once in Trest but… living clockwork tech is outlawed for everyone except the Proph—"

"Excuse me," the clockwork man's accented baritone interrupted, "I don't appreciate being referred to in the third person when I'm right in the room."

Jim leapt from his seat and exclaimed, "It spoke!"

"HE spoke," Henry corrected him.

Captain Rychist laughed and turned to Henry. "Seeing people react to you never gets old. It's like a child seeing some new wonder for the first time."

Jim frowned and thought, *most children don't see something like this in their lifetime.*

"Not too many marvels out in the wastes, huh?" the captain asked.

Before Jim could respond, Henry interrupted again, "As the captain said, my name is Henry. Yes, living clockwork tech is highly illegal. Of course, that doesn't stop Her Royal 'Tyranical'ness from owning it." The contempt in his tin voice was sharp. "However, I am the property of no one, man or woman."

Jim couldn't quite place the accent. And the symbols on the mobility ball... there was definitely a familiarity to it. He looked into Henry's glowing blue eyes and said, "I didn't mean to offend you but, uh, how old are you?"

"Oh boy," The captain rolled her eyes.

Henry's eyes brightened, "Oh! I'm so glad you asked!" The tray was set down quickly with a clunk on the antique desk. The lid of the coffee pot fell onto the tray. He rapped a metal hand against his chest and replied, "This chassis is only ninety seven, but I believe my ether cube, my heart if you will, to be over ten thousand years old!"

The captain raised a hand and shook her head. "Please Henry. This poor man can only take so much in his first day among the clouds. Let's not fill his head full of your stories of speculation. At least, not today."

"They're hardly stories, captain," he replied defensively. "The ether cubes contain the essence of our progenitors. Essentially, I'm one of those ancients, or at least, I was created by them, and will prove it, someday."

The captain shook her head. "Listen, there's still much for Jim to learn. Perhaps we can reserve your... history lesson for another time."

A loud bell ringing somewhere outside cut her words short.

The captain was already on her feet when Harol burst through their door. His brass goggles were pushed onto his thick cotton flight cap. In his hand, he still held the welding torch. "Sorry for interruptin'. Captain, raiders are approachin' from the northwest. Lookout reports at least three dozen of 'em. All in Firebugs. We got about five minutes before things get interestin'."

The captain's jovial expression disappeared. She pulled an antiquated matchlock pistol from her desk and tucked it into her belt behind her back. With fire in her eyes, she shouted the command.

"BATTLESTATIONS!"

Chapter III

Tempest

"Jim, up the J ropes!" The captain shouted.

"But I-"

"We can talk later, if we make it," the captain replied as she pushed him through the cabin door.

Jim rushed toward the nearest fanned rope ladder. They were called Jacob's ladders but more often referred to as J ropes. Behind him, he could still hear the captain barking orders to the crew, "Get on a turngun! Henry, give the order to take us up higher. Their wings are shit at high altitude. Harol, where are the twins? I need them..."

Captain Rychist's voice trailed off as she disappeared up the forecastle stairs and out of view.

The crew was scrambling in every direction. Dozens of them hastily ascended J ladders hanging from the balloon. Jim ran for the nearest one. The captain's earlier words played over in his head, "I just hope you don't have a fear of heights."

Jim scurried up the ropes, trying to ignore the world thousands of meters below him. His bones shook as a loud thrumming started from below deck. The lazy *thump thump thump* of the ship's propellers quickened until they droned steadily. Wisps of steam poured out from belowdecks as the coal fed engine hissed and roared. More alarm bells were ringing, and shouts carried upward from deep within the ship.

Focusing on the ropes ahead and above, Jim continued his climb. The balloon's pull on the J ropes kept them tight, but it didn't stop his mind from playing games with his senses. The fear of a rope giving way and tossing him into the abyss lingered between his animal and logical brain, threatening to petrify his body mid-climb.

The Liberator had already begun its ascent. The pleasant white cloud sea below them was now a distant blanket. As they pushed up into a higher, much colder layer, a chilly fog engulfed the ship. The sky seemed to darken as they rose, while the deep thrumming rhythm of steam being belched into the balloon gave the impression that he was climbing up the ribs of a giant leviathan. Jim shook the image from his head and tried to focus on the task at hand.

The hull soon disappeared behind the bulk of the balloon as he quickened his pace. His heart was pounding in his chest, and he slowed to allow his lungs to catch up with his body's demand in the rarified air.

One step. Then another and another. Soon, the clouds below were replaced by the curve of the balloon's canvas as he scrambled the last few meters to the top.

Moments later, catapulting out from the sides of the Liberator — five, eight, ten fighters burst forth. They were heavy Dragonfly variants, large two man fighters used mainly against ground targets. The dual wings would also serve them at such a high altitude, hopefully providing an advantage against the oncoming firebug squadron Harol had warned of.

Dragonflies took their name from a nearly identical resemblance to the bug commonly found around the water supplies of most desert oases. The heavy fighters used a dizzying array of gears linked to a yellow ether cube to beat their quad wings in perfect sync, mimicking the insect in everything but size. Even the sound of one flying nearby was strikingly similar to the real insect.

The Marauders' Firebugs, on the other hand, carried only a single high refire turngun in the nose and a single pair of rapidly beating mechanical wings. Also powered by yellow ether cubes, as all aircraft were, they were fairly harmless alone, but in swarms, they could be deadly with their low caliber, fast firing nose guns. Somewhere to the northwest, one such swarm was coming their way.

The curve of the balloon began to level out, and soon he was on his feet. Jim stumbled toward the nearest emplacement, trying to catch his breath as he went along. The thinning air was wreaking havoc on his burning lungs and only added to his disorientation.

What the hell am I doing here? he asked himself. Since he'd woken up, he felt as if he'd been dragged along through a wild fever dream. The ship, the captain, the clockwork man, and now... this.

BOOM! A peal of thunder burst through the clouds and slammed into him like a hammer, robbing him of breath for a moment. Jim shook his head clear, as clear as he could anyhow. Whatever this was, he was here now and would do his part to survive.

Ahead, his turngun sat atop a small wooden platform that had been fastened to the thick balloon canvas. Surrounding it was a two layer high sandbag wall. The brass contraption had dual handcranks hooked up to a gearing system that rotated eight barrels arranged around a core. Ammo and powder bags dropped downward through separate hoppers into the top barrel, each bag carefully measured so as not to jam the loading mechanism.

With each turn of the crank, a flint cap was struck, igniting the tiny powder bag and sending the spheroid projectile toward its target. Of course, fighters and other powered contraptions did this all automatically thanks to the power flowing from their ether cubes. Unfortunately, this turngun would require Jim power, limited though it may be.

Shuddering and releasing an enormous belch of steam, the ship jolted as they reached their target altitude. Jim quickly grabbed a pair of brass-rimmed flight goggles hanging from one of the cranks and fixed them tightly to his head. The rims were lined with matted material: gamal hair, he guessed. They had a set of drop lenses for distant viewing, ready to be pulled down at the wearer's discretion.

Over the commotion below and the rapidly oncoming storm, he could make out the shouts of Captain Rychist. He couldn't hear what she was saying, but there was a tension in her voice. If he were to guess, he was almost certain it was fear.

The air was intolerably cold, especially to Jim's desert-acclimated sensibilities. He realized how underdressed he was compared to the rest of the crew members he had seen. Suddenly, a warm cloud of released steam passed over him and provided brief respite, though leaving him wet and cold a few seconds later. The thick grey cloud was acrid with the smell of degraded black crystal and coal.

Jim grabbed the leather shoulder harness hanging from the gun chair and strapped himself in. Through the cold metal bucket seat of his emplacement, he could feel every bump and vibration from the ship below. He suspected the platform was anchored to one or more of the steel frames that gave the balloon its streamlined shape.

The Liberator's squadron of Dragonflies circled around it as they formed a perimeter in the air. Their quickly heating yellow cores reflected against the trails of white that streamed behind each fighter as they corkscrewed in tight formation. He imagined that from a distance, the Liberator must appear to be wearing a golden halo of steam.

But something far more sinister drew his gaze. Against the horizon a wholly artificial, wholly deadly, black cloud raced toward the ship. Peals of thunder announced their coming doom as white lightning snaked throughout the unnatural vapor. Within the darkness, yellow dots darted left and right appearing for seconds before retreating into the veil.

"By the Gods, they have a prime of air in there!" came a cry from the emplacement nearest to him.

"What's a prime!?" Jim shouted back, but the commotion of Dragonflies and an approaching maelstrom drowned his voice in the chaos. The storm was nearly upon them, rumbling like an avalanche as it approached. The man shouted something and pointed toward the cloud. Jim couldn't make out the words, but the fear in the man's face told him everything he needed to know.

He fought the urge to unstrap, dive down, and hide behind his meager sandbag wall. Fear weakened his grip on the weapon's cranks as he stepped on the right control pedal. The small dais beneath him hissed as steam from the balloon escaped to engage the gearing, turning him in the direction of the pedal.

He released the control pedal as his weapon leveled toward the storm. From head to toe, his body tightened in preparation for the unknown. *What the hell am I doing here?* He thought. *I don't even know these people.*

At that moment, he wanted very much to be back on his ship. It may have been a barely floating piece of junk, but it was far closer to the ground.

Accompanying the ever present fear of small spaces, he had apparently picked up a fresh fear of heights. His heart fluttered under a wave of anxiety.

Four seconds.

In one fluid motion, a wing of four Dragonflies broke from the perimeter and charged the oncoming storm for a pre-emptive strike.

Three seconds.

Fearlessly, the fighters plunged into the grey wall. A veil of lightning burned their shadows across his eyesight as the cloud flashed images of the Dragonflies firing their weapons into the swarm of Firebugs.

Two seconds.

For a moment, everything was silent. Jim held his breath.

One second.

Time stalled.

Hit.

Jim's world erupted. Underneath him, the bag rippled and steel shrieked. The storm slammed into their ship like a wall of stone. Instantly, the sky had gone dark. Clouds of black swirled around him. Any warmth he had retained was washed away in sheets of pounding rain.

Again, he could hear the Dragonflies… and countless Firebugs. The drone of fighters was almost overwhelming. Crashes of thunder, clanging of alarm bells, engines, and turngun fire. The air was laden with noise.

An image darted across his vision, but then it was gone. Jim's eyes shifted left and right. Despite the deafening noise, he could hear his own heavy breathing. His head throbbed with each pounding heartbeat. Suddenly, there it was.

The Firebug moved so quickly, he wasn't sure how its pilot could remain conscious. Flying sideways, the insect-shaped craft cut through the air, firing its low caliber nose gun at the emplacement next to him. Though the sound of the tempest was disorienting, he could see a young man shouting in defiance as he turned the cranks furiously and fired on the small craft.

Coming to his senses, and not wanting to be discluded, Jim gripped the cranks of his own turngun. *POP POP POP POP*. The pitiful sound of his hand-cranked weapon would have been cause for humor if his life weren't hanging in the balance.

Four more emplacements followed. Although hand-cranked turnguns were notoriously inaccurate, teams of them firing at a single close range target were effective, even if by accident.

Jim's shots missed wide and to the right. His neighbor fared better, scoring multiple hits on one of the translucent insect-shaped wings. Already struggling for lift in the thin air, the first Firebug rolled quickly out of control, bouncing off the balloon once and disappearing into the blackness below.

Again, the young man was shouting at Jim, this time pointing to a latch on his own gun. It took him a moment to make the connection. Jim probed his turngun and found a similar lever. He grabbed hold of the small bar and pulled it back with a satisfying *click*. A third, much smaller container, located between the ammo and charge hoppers marked Incendiary, dropped its first round into the chamber.

The next Firebug came straight at them, cresting over the canvas horizon from somewhere below the bow of the ship. It dipped and rose as it fought to maintain course so high above its flight ceiling. For a moment, it appeared, veiled in shadow as an exploding fighter behind it turned the grey clouds orange.

Again, the guns spit their fury as fast as their operators could turn the cranks. Lines of red traced the sky from the six turnguns atop the balloon. Each sought out the enemy craft. The Firebug tucked and bounced in random directions. Its lack of control just made the work of the turngun operators more difficult.

Jim was panting as he poured his strength into the hand cranks of his gun. Balls of white and red fire spit forth. Clouds of warm gunsmoke brushed his flight goggles, often impeding his line of sight. The shots missed again as they left trails across his vision.

His emplacement finally drew the attention of the fighter. The pilot wrestled control of the Firebug and turned. The fighter hovered for a hair of a second before dipping forward toward Jim's position. Lines of fire from the other emplacements followed behind as it charged.

Turngun rounds ripped through the surface of the balloon toward Jim's exposed position. He continued to fire his weapon. Jim's muscles burned from the effort, or lack of oxygen, or both.

The buzzing of metal through air grew closer, and the holes in the balloon rushed toward his emplacement. At the last moment, Jim slipped out of his harness and dove for cover. His turngun continued on momentum and fired two more shots.

Jim rolled onto his back just in time to see the smouldering craft rip through the air overhead. A small section of its fuselage had been ignited by an incendiary round. He wasn't sure if the hit had been scored by his unmanned weapon, or one of the emplacements, but he didn't have time to consider either.

Suddenly, what appeared to me a small line of smoke burst into a fire within the body of the craft. The glass cockpit glowed orange as a torrent of burning destruction pressurized the small space. At once, the glass cockpit exploded into a million shards and the smoking body of the very surprised pilot was ejected out in a flaming trail.

For a moment, Jim watched in confusion. *Those shots barely penetrated the fighter*, he thought. He turned to see the gunner in the emplacement next to his standing with arms outstretched toward the staggering fighter. Even through the darkness around them, Jim could see the boy's arms blackening as the explosion of internal power took its toll in his body.

A fire Awakened! Jim realized.

The burning fighter crashed into the tail section of the balloon, bouncing end over end, taking a piece of the top rudder with it before disappearing below. Dropping to his knees, the gunner smiled, exhausted from the effort, and collapsed behind his sandbag wall.

Jim didn't have time to check on the fallen Awakened warrior. Suddenly, a burst of air knocked him down. Above, three Dragonflies droned past at high speed. Their discipline was commendable as they crossed the sky, smoking tail guns making quick work of the closest pursuing Firebugs.

Jim felt the ship lurch beneath him as it dropped. Dozens of holes were leaking steam now. Some of the gunners had scrambled out of their harnesses to patch the punctures, but he doubted it would make much difference. The air rushed by him and his stomach knotted as they descended.

More aircraft fell into the blackness in smouldering ruins. Other gunners were out of their harnesses now, contributing their own Awakened fire to the destruction. Victory was starting to feel like a real possibility. Burning wounds in some of the nearest enemy aircraft were quickly transformed into gaping geysers of flame, as fire awakened manipulated the small flames into pillars of destruction.

Next, many things went wrong.

The clouds ignited in a white glow as bolts of lightning unceremoniously obliterated the three nearest dragonflies. Their fuselages were torn in two as if by an invisible butcher's blade, sending blood, bone, and machine into the darkened abyss.

More lightning tore emplacements from the balloon, opening up more holes in the already damaged structure. Precious lift steam was leaking through huge gashes now as the ship began to freefall.

Below, fireballs and gunfire reached out desperately in every direction. The fighters had broken through the ship's thinning perimeter of Dragonflies and were moving in for a massed attack. Crewmen were sacrificing themselves, using far more awakened power than they were meant to.

The awakened threw fireballs and some manipulated jagged bolts of lightning at the oncoming craft. It was all a hopeless effort to hold back the enemy for a few more tragic seconds. One after another, men and women with blackened arms fell unconscious onto the deck as their bodies were spent.

Shouts of terror and anguish filled the sky. Overspent Awakened crew continued to drop. Still others fell to enemy turngun fire, their lives extinguished in blood and horror. Fire and lightning burned paths of destruction in every direction. The ship's crew descended on the ten pound cannons, firing grapeshot in a futile effort to score a few lucky hits on the Firebugs.

Jim even spotted a pair holding a pop-grapple, a weapon meant for boarding other large vessels. They fired the compressed air grapple launcher at a passing Firebug but missed by a dozen meters.

For a moment, hopelessness lay thick in the air. The crew was breaking, their terror palpable. They were trapped in hell itself, plunging together to their certain deaths. But there was something else.

Deep within his mind, a presence spoke. Beneath him, the rocks cried out *We are near!* But not in ordinary words. It was instinct, given voice: an experience peculiar to the awakened, Jim would come to find.

Somehow, he could hear it, feel the earth as they plummeted toward it. The ship was erupting in a steam cloud as the engine room released all reserves into the balloon, struggling to keep the floundering vessel airborne. The ship was dangerously close to the ground now. He couldn't see it, but he felt it was near. The deck jolted again as their death dive became a freefall.

Not knowing what to do, he lifted his arms skyward just as the young fire Awakened had done. He closed his eyes and concentrated. *What do I do next?* he thought as the feeling of approaching doom quickened his already pounding heart.

Nothing.

Just the rocks shouting out.

But then…

A feeling of peace overcame him. Jim took a breath and exhaled slowly. The rapid thumping of the airship's engines crawled to a steady *whoosh whoosh whoosh*. Time seemed to slow with each breath.

Jim opened his eyes, slowly, in a half dream. Suddenly, he could see himself suspended above the ground just as he had during his awakening. Somewhere inside, he knew that he was still standing on the balloon canvas, or at least his body was, but he was an observer above the scene now, serene in the sky.

In his mind's eye, the air stilled. He and his Awakened crewmates were floating above a rocky ridgeline intersected with the Great Dune Sea. Glowing figures ran about in slow motion beneath him. The ship was a looming shadow with small points of light occupying its decks. He worked out that the bright figures were the life forces of each Awakened crew member, and the ship, an inanimate object, was little more than a lifeless shadow.

Some lights shone a deep red, others a dull orange. Still others glowed in various shades of yellow and white. Fire and air Awakened, he realized. Jim looked down at his own body. Unlike the others, it was black. Yet, it glowed. It both absorbed light and emitted it.

The best he could ever describe it thereafter was that it looked "Like an obsidian rock with a purple aura surrounding it," but Jim always felt that the description blunted the true brilliance of its appearance, and henceforth ceased attempting to explain.

Perplexed by all he was seeing, he cleared the questions from his mind and returned his attention to the world unfolding beneath him. In the sand below, he could see every living thing. Tiny stars of life shone brightly upon the ground. Like him, the dunes were dark, but glowed with a faint aura of deep violets.

He shifted his gaze upwards. Even the enemy pilots had a glow. One of them was particularly bright. *Is that the 'prime?'* he wondered.

The rock and sand were shouting to him now, *WE ARE HERE!*
COMMAND US! Above, four remaining Dragonflies danced a suicidal ballet
with scores of Firebugs. The pilots fought with remarkable courage, but their
struggle was ending. Two of them were falling out of formation, trailing
greasy black smoke.

The rocks and sand beneath him were screaming for his attention,
COMMAND US! YOU MUST! DO IT NOW!

Silence again. Jim closed his eyes. "Go," was all he could say.

The earth rumbled as it rolled and rippled beneath the ship. They had
landed, somehow intact. A testament to a well-trained, or perhaps, very
lucky crew. Although he couldn't see it, he could feel the ship buck and list
beneath his feet as the last of the lifting steam escaped the balloon.

The tumult grew to a crescendo.

Pillars of sand and rock launched skyward from the ground.
Explosions ripped through the silence as boulders, sand, and stone erased
the nearest Firebugs from the sky. All around him, the lights of those below
seemed to brighten. Above, the enemy points of light were blinking out
of existence.

Fire awakened crew joined the maelstrom above with their own efforts,
directing the explosive fire to the remaining ships. The last conscious air
awakened on their ship added to the fight, sending the explosions
backward with tremendous gusts of wind.

As each ship was engulfed, the fireball grew, feeding even greater
destruction into the next.

With their demise fast approaching, the remaining Firebugs broke
pursuit and retreated north. His second sight began to fade. He willed the
sand to engulf them, but his awakened control had reached its end and the
sand barely rippled.

Soon, the mechanical buzzing of enemy fighters faded into nothingness.

Jim's senses slowly returned to him. The air around was warm, dry,
familiar. The sound of wind through Manzatrees and shifting sand
welcomed him from below. He opened weary eyes to a slanted view of the
world. His body was resting under a pile of strewn sandbags and rubble.
Next to him, the Liberator's balloon was deflating in a final cloud of acrid
steam.

The superstructure, normally hidden within, was poking through a
much deflated canvas like the ribs of a starving animal.

Joy, relief, and sorrow overcame him. As the last of his power left, the
toll for his act came due. Nausea rolled through his stomach followed by
a deep ache throughout his body. He raised his blackened hands in front
of his face. Then, for the second time that week, the warm comfort of
unconsciousness took him.

Chapter IV
Sand Again

"You know, Jim, you sleep too much," said a soft alto voice, cutting through the darkness of his sleep. "Henry, get him cleaned up and fill him in. I'll be with the engineers down in the steam room."

There was a sound of rapid light steps on wood and the metal creak of hinges turning. The sharp sound pulled him from his sleep.

A second voice replied with a familiar metallic baritone, "Well, I'd be sleeping too. I mean that's twice in a handful of days you've used Awakened power. And at that intensity, well, frankly he should be very dead by now."

Jim shook his head and blinked his eyes. As he sat upright, familiar walls took shape around him. There was the same hatch door and bowing ceilings. "This place again," he whispered through parched lips.

"OOF!"

Henry slapped him on the back with a much too hard metallic hand. "This place indeed! Be happy that you're in the infirmary and not buried in a shallow grave. You pretty much saved us all back there, by the way."

"Huh? What did I… oh right," Jim stopped, suddenly remembering the events of the afternoon before. He probed his body for bandages, but this time, it seemed he'd escaped his explosion of Awakened power relatively uninjured.

He looked over to Henry. A young man of no more than eighteen was standing next to him, looking down. "Hey, uhh Jim, I wanted to thank you for your help back there on the topside. Not to mention the whole exploding ground thing. You're gonna have to tell me how you did that some time. Well… how you did it and survived."

The boy next to Henry was gaunt and short. Or it could have just been the contrast between the lumbering clockwork man and the small teen, he wasn't sure.

Jim's attention was fixed on his hair, however. The dirty blonde mess was cut into an awkward upside-down bowl shape around his head. It was completely out of place for a crewman, or anyone for that matter. In fact, Jim couldn't help but feel that it was downright comical. Despite his headache, he had to suppress a startled snort.

"My name is Sasha," the young man said.

Jim stared at him, still trying to hold his composure.

"And no," Sasha continued. "I didn't choose this ridiculous haircut." He nearly crossed his eyes as he looked up at his straight bangs, only adding to the humerous effect.

The miserable looking Sasha sighed, "I'll be happy to tell the whole story later. For now, the cap'n wants us to get underway. She estimates a week or so of repairs on the Liberator. That doesn't leave us much time to get to Rock Bottom and back."

"Rock Bottom?" Jim asked.

"Yes, the unaligned city southeast of Vigilance Oasis," Sasha replied.

"No, I know, but why go there?" Jim said.

Henry spoke first, "That little aerial display cost us dearly in black-crystal reserves. We barely have enough remaining to lift this old tub again, let alone fly to safety. Thankfully, we keep a couple sloops in the hold for hunting and scavenging."

"Sloops? How much storage space does this ship have?" Jim wondered aloud.

Henry shrugged and replied, "With a little creative engineering, our people worked out a way to store the sloops belowdecks. It isn't as complicated as it sounds. We use a metal locking pivot joint to fold the masts down, and sloops are tiny, little more than dinghys."

Jim opened his mouth to speak, but Henry continued, "While you were getting your beauty sleep, the crew reassembled both ships. The first just left for the eastern wastes to do some hunting around the base of Mount Anvil. That leaves us with a simple trader's errand. Exchange some goods, get some crystal, and get back."

"Why me?" Jim asked.

This time, Sasha spoke, "You are a trader aren't you? We assumed, as someone who sails the dunes, you've made port in Rock Bottom a few times."

Jim nodded. Although he preferred to avoid civilization when possible, he'd anchored in Rock Bottom on more than a few occasions and knew the area well. Jim had learned early on that every good trader needs contacts. He had at least a few in most free ports, and one particularly reliable person in Rock Bottom.

"Yeah, I've been there," Jim admitted. "So, who is going? The captain?" he asked, hoping his anticipation at that prospect was well-veiled.

"Sasha and I will be accompanying you. The best company around in my opinion. Captain's got plenty to do here," Henry said with another unwelcome slap on the back.

Jim sighed inwardly. *Stuck with a kid with a goofy haircut and a chatty clockwork man. Well, at least Rock Bottom is a free city. Less taxes, and better meade.*

"I really think you should find someone else," he said. "I should be here helping with repairs."

"Speaking of repairs," Henry interrupted, "I believe the captain is outside conducting a few of her own as we speak. Perhaps you should go have a chat with her."

"Fine," Jim said with a shrug as he stood up and adjusted his shirt.

He couldn't quite hear Henry whisper to Sasha, "This ought to be entertaining."

It was shaping up to be another typical day on the burning sands of Ruin. The sun had barely peeked over the horizon, casting long shadows off the dunes, and already the heat was stifling. The morning whisper of the winds sent the endless golden dunes along their daily shapeshifting course.

Jim slid carefully down the listed topdeck of the Liberator. After bounding off of the side rail, he landed with a thud on the shifting sand. Already, the air had gone brown with the kicked up dust of the morning. He secured his keffiyeh to his face and turned to take stock of the damage.

The giant wounded wood beast that was the Liberator stretched to the corners of his vision. It lay on its starboard side. Part of its railing had already disappeared under the sand below. Across the deck, hundreds of ropes were tightly stretched from their anchor points to the balloon frame which also lay to starboard.

The balloon was twice the size of the hull, and though it was deflated, the skeleton of its frame held it in place. Jim could see dozens perhaps hundreds of places where the low caliber rounds of the Firebug's turnguns had penetrated the canvas.

Already, the crew had begun their patch work. It appeared to be all hands on deck as over a hundred crewmen went about their tasks. Some sewed small cloth patches on the balloon while others hammered away with replacement boards on the largest gaps in the wooden hull. Jim could hear the curses of mechanics somewhere deep in the boiler room and they banged and wrenched the complicated machinery that normally kept the Liberator far above the sands.

"Harol, slow it down or it's going to drop!" Jim heard the familiar voice of the doctor. He spotted the man on the port side of the ship, straddling the railing so as to avoid a lengthy tumble across the deck and into the sand. His arms waved violently as he hurled the occasional obscenity.

Jim jogged around the length of the ship, preferring the sand to the precarious deck. As he rounded the bow, he could see what the doctor had been yelling about. Suspended from a pair of ropes as thick as his sword arm was a small wooden sloop. The ropes ran into two large steel-spoked wheels that were attached to an iron steam engine. The engine belched clouds of black coal smoke and steam as it hissed and groaned against the weight of the vessel, small though it was.

The sloop looked to be no more than fifteen meters long, but it was proving to be quite difficult to dislodge, pushing the steam engine to its limits. Atop the groaning mass of metal was Harol, the lead deckhand. He strained as he pressed an engaging lever forward. Nearby on the sand, the twin boys Jim had spotted the day earlier were shoveling coal from an open sack into the engine. On its side in black lettering were the words, 50 Bushel Coal - Alliance Navy."

Considering the Warlord Alliance was hundreds of kilometers to the south, and they most certainly didn't share, Jim guessed there was an interesting story there.

"Ugh, we should have salvaged that ether engine at the last grab. I hate these steam divas. Always giving me trouble."

From the railing, the doctor shouted down, "Now now Alia, you know it's bad luck to insult an engine to its face."

Jim tilted his head sideways and spotted Captain Rychist on the far side of the engine. She lay on her back and was covered in black coal streaks and even blacker grease. A keffiyeh covered her sweat-sheened face and was already blackened from breathing in coal dust.

"Uhh, captain?" Jim said, but the hissing of the engine drowned out his words. He cleared his throat and tried again. "Captain, concerning this uhhh journey, to Rock Bottom." It was no use. Between the screeching of metal, the howling of the wind, and the captain's protestations, he went unheard.

"Gods of hell, damn this overweight shitpile," Alia cursed as she banged on the engine with what looked like a wooden mallet.

Jim saw an opportunity.

"Can I help at all?" he shouted over the commotion.

Suddenly, the captain missed a stroke and smashed her thumb with the mallet. "AAAA! Dammit Jim, you scared the hell out of me. How long have you been there?"

"I uhh," Jim scratched at the back of his neck. "Sorry about that. I…"

The captain sighed. "No no, it's fine. I'm just… it's fine." She sat up and rubbed her thumb. "It's this winch engine. Normally, it's more than sufficient at winching the sloops out of the hangars, but the ship is forty degrees to starboard right now. That adds a lot of strain."

From atop the engine, Harol's face peeked out. "She's leakin' steam like a wounded animal, captain. We gotta get that boilerplate locked down or the sloop's gonna drop."

"Could you use an extra pair of hands?" Jim suggested, reaching for the mallet that was laying in the sand.

"Step aside, stringbean," the captain cut him off. She reached down for the spanner and removed it from the last boilerplate nut. High pressure steam continued to pour out of the hole. Carefully, she turned the spanner the opposite direction and fastened it to the nut so that its handle was at a slight incline.

"No offence, Jim, but you know nothing about this kind of thing. I've been fixing steam engines since before you ever stepped foot on a vessel. Observe."

She took a few steps back, indicating for Jim to step aside. He did, and just in time, as the captain ran full speed toward the engine. She vaulted off the sand at the last minute with a grunt and sailed through the air before landing with both feet on the spanner handle.

The combination of speed and her full body weight made the nut spin with a loud *RRRRRRT.*

"And THAT is how you tighten a stubborn nut!" she said with a mocking bow. The twins stopped for a moment to clap and Harol rolled his eyes.

"Ahh, the Alia maneuver," the doctor shouted down. "Best avoid her using it on you, lad."

The captain walked over to Jim panting. "It's not that I don't think you could've done it," she said, her voice calming, "but you've been bedridden almost from the moment we met. I'd rather you save your strength for the trip to Rock Bottom. Now go and get Henry and Sasha. You have at least a few days' journey ahead of you."

"Sorry, captain," Jim began, "I was just trying to-"

"I know. Now hop to it."

"Actually, captain," Henry said, appearing as if from nowhere, "Jim here has something he'd like to say to you. Isn't that right Jim?" Sasha and Henry had been standing silently by stifling snickers.

"Is that so?" Alia asked.

"I uhhh yes, miss... Uhh ma'am.. I mean..."

"Captain, if you please mister Jim."

"Yes, Captain," Jim replied. "It's just. Well, this trip to Rock Bottom. Perhaps you could better use my talents here?"

Alia crossed her arms. It left another black streak on what were once white sleeves as her coal dust covered hands locked into place. "And what talents are those exactly?"

"The talent to watch you fix things," Henry shouted over the wind. Both he and Sasha were now barely containing their laughter.

Alia seemed unimpressed.

Jim's heart skipped a beat as he fumbled with the words to say. "No, no, no. I could help you with other things like... like..."

"Like perhaps doing your laundry," Henry shouted. Now, he and Sasha couldn't hold it back. They burst into laughter.

"Alright, that's enough out of you two," the captain snapped. "Enough with the schoolboy shenanigans. Go prep the sloop before I forget to pack a sail and make you both pull the thing like pack animals."

Sasha scurried off. Henry gave a quick mock salute across his chest which let out a loud clang. "Right away, ma'am!" he shouted.

"Don't you 'ma'am' me, you scrap pile of…"

But Henry had already made a hasty retreat, giggling as he did.

"As for you," the captain said, turning an icy glare back to Jim. "Perhaps you're not used to a command structure, so I'll let this infraction pass without subjecting you to a fate similar to the young mister Sasha."

Jim tried to appear defiant. But his stiff stance nearly landed him sideways in the sand as he lost his balance.

"When I task you, or anyone in the crew for that matter with something, you can consider it an order. This isn't the Alliance or Federation military, but I do expect my crew to follow my orders so long as they serve under me."

"Yes, captain," Jim replied. He tried to imitate the salute that Henry had given.

"And dammit don't salute me. I just told you, we aren't the military. Henry's just being an annoying ass. A right he's earned and you have not. When or if you earn that right, I'll let you know, but in the meantime, you will follow orders, or be put off the ship."

For a fraction of a moment, Jim considered making a joke about the current state of the ship, but the determined stare of the captain dissuaded him of that particular opportunity for humor.

"Yes, captain," he replied.

"Now," she said, "head to the sloop and help Henry and Sasha get her underway."

Jim nodded and trotted toward the sloop. Behind him, her face mostly hidden under her keffiyeh, Alia was grinning.

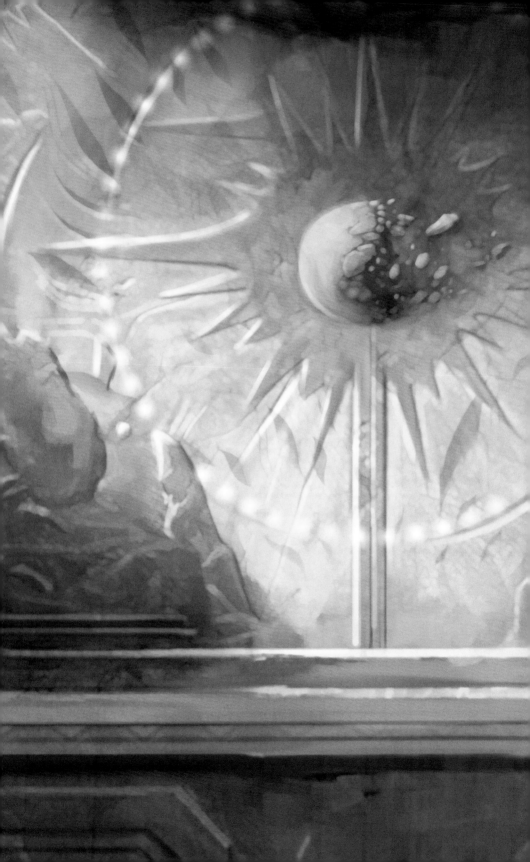

Chapter V
Broken Moon

The twilight winds were finally stilling. Night was setting in, and the broken Moon began its slow crawl across the sky. This far south in the desert there was no folliage, just sand and rock. Stealing a quiet moment, which was quite rare around Henry, Jim closed his eyes and breathed in the desert air.

At night, the temperatures in the Great Dune Sea shifted from a raging inferno to a slightly more tolerable smoulder. Still, it was a welcome relief. Most of the day consisted of sailing work paired with baking under the unforgiving sun.

The day's journey had been long and hot, but Jim was glad it had been by landship and not Gamails: the large-horned hairy pack animals were reliable, but smelled terrible, and were not known for their speed, or for being very cooperative.

Throughout the day, each crew member had taken turns above deck to keep the ship pointed in the right direction. Henry had volunteered for a longer shift since apparently clockwork men were "less affected by environmental conditions" as he put it. Finally, as the sun had set, they'd found port on a sandstone mesa and tore apart some empty crates for firewood.

As Jim chewed on the last of his seeds, he shifted. A question had been biting at him all day. Finally, he sighed and asked, "Ok, I have to know. What's with the haircut, kid?"

Henry's luminescent body stuck out against the growing pitch black of night as he too turned to Sasha. "The man finally speaks! Yes, please do tell our friend. How in Ruin's depths did you come across that monstrosity?"

Jim couldn't be certain in the dim glow of the fire but he was pretty sure Sasha was blushing. The young man sighed, "It's a punishment."

Jim probed further.

"A punishment?"

He tried again.

"Umm..for what?"

"For theft."

Jim waited. Finally, Sasha continued. "I came aboard a few weeks ago, after they raided the Tanhar Monastery. I'd only been there a few months, so the brainwashing hadn't been completed."

"How did they, the priests I mean, find you in the first place?" Jim asked.

Sasha sighed again, "One of those nosy priests found me in the back alleys of Togsov City. Unlike you, I never had a big awakening. Chances are, unless I was somehow in a situation of life and death, I never would have."

Jim motioned for Sasha to continue.

"You see, unlike you, I never experienced a natural awakening. Some of the more powerful air Awakened have a sort of ability to detect the potential in people and draw it out within those monasteries. Long story short, they caught me, brought me north and began my re-education."

"Ok, now back to the haircut." Henry prodded. His tone of voice hinted to Jim that he already knew the answer.

Sasha continued, "I was only a few months into it when Captain Rychist and the Liberator came along. They rescued me and a few other Awakened acolytes from the school. I became a crewman and was brought into the fold."

Sheepishly, he added, "Growing up on the streets, you learn certain things. Pick up habits and so on. You know the saying, 'old habits die hard'?"

Jim nodded.

"Well, about a week ago we were all eating dinner in the mess hall, and I noticed an untouched bowl of cactus fruit and allta pudding just sitting on a corner table. It looked delicious. I waited a few minutes and, when nobody sat down in front of it… well… I sorta maybe swiped it. I figured, 'finder's keeper's', you know?"

Jim raised an eyebrow and asked, "They punished you for taking unclaimed food?"

Henry was glowing a few shades brighter now, barely containing his laughter. "Oh that wasn't just any bowl of pudding, my friend. When they caught him, our young friend here learned that it belonged to someone you really don't want to rankle!"

Sasha continued, somber, "Yeah… it was apparently a special treat for Captain Rychist from the chef. He'd been working on it all day. I uhh… stole her favorite dessert."

"So," Jim cleared his throat to cover a laugh, "I should look forward to such a haircut if I piss her off?"

Sasha chortled, "Nah, more likely she will simply knock you on your ass. Steal a bowl of her pudding though? She'll use that bowl for your very own haircut such as you see here. Oh, and she'll make half the crew watch while it happens." He tried to look up at his hair, again appearing cross eyed as he did so.

"Yes, I should have warned the young one," Henry said between laughs, "The captain is really fond of food. You committed the most heinous crime in her eyes."

All three of them had a good laugh. It was the first time Jim had laughed like that in a long while. He stroked his chin, musing to the others, "The lesson here is, if you steal the captain's food, go for a much larger bowl."

Their laughter echoed off the lonely rocks as they continued to share stories late into the night.

It was almost midnight. The broken Moon was high in the sky. Its many small pieces danced and sparkled against a beautiful tapestry of stars as it slowly made its way to the horizon.

Jim had always been a creature of the night. Even after the most exhausting of days, he'd found himself laying out on the deck of his rickety cutter watching the sky turn slowly by, wondering at its mysteries. The desert may have dulled his manners, but never his mind.

He wandered back to the sloop, leaving his comrades asleep around the glowing embers of the fire. According to Henry, clockwork men did indeed sleep and dream "Just as humans do." Henry's snores sounded more like a light brushing of metal on metal. Jim grinned as he wondered, *how does he snore? He doesn't even have lungs.*

Although anchored, the sloop still bobbed in the gentle night air. He always felt more comfortable on the deck of a ship than the sands of the wastes. It was as if the air carried him from the trappings of civilization and closer to some deeper understanding of the natural world around him. He made his way up the bobbing gangplank and found a spot of planking that looked relatively flat. Unrolling his bedroll, he lay back and watched the stars.

His eyes were growing heavy and, finally, sleep began to take him. The gentle rocking of the ship and the warm air on his skin began to usher him quietly out of consciousness.

"The desert has a certain beauty to it, does it not?"

Jim shot up to his feet and reached for the scimitar hanging from his belt. The unfamiliar voice set him instantly on edge. Looking around the murky darkness, he spotted a small figure sitting on the starboard rail of the bobbing ship.

Through dim starlight and pale beams cast by the broken Moon, he made out the crooked grinning teeth of an old man. The person spoke in a raspy voice, "Don't worry, boy, I intend no harm. Besides, what could a man of my physical condition do?"

His voice was as dry and ancient like the desert. Something in the tone though set Jim at ease. The adrenaline burned out, and his quaking muscles steadied.

"Who are you? What do you want?" Jim whispered warily, still unwilling to sheath his weapon.

"Nobody special. Not anymore, unlike yourself," the man replied as a bony finger protruded from his ragged tunic. "As for what I want, there are many things. The usual forlorn desires. My youth back, second chances, happiness, family. You know, the nostalgic longings of most old men." A wheezing chuckle escaped the stranger's throat.

Something in the man's tone conveyed a sharp intelligence. He sounded old enough to be one foot in the grave, but somehow his voice showed unnatural youth.

Jim took a breath and tried again, "What I mean is, what do you want from me? And how are you... alive way out here?"

The old man slid easily to a standing position from his perch on the railing. His aged body moved with the grace of someone twenty years his junior. As he neared, Jim caught a glimpse of a long, unkempt beard of white. The man's face was wrinkled and worn.

It was the eyes that intrigued him. Blue as the midday sky, they seemed to sparkle in the starlight. There was an awareness in them and a stark focus. The more Jim studied him, the more the man appeared to be a jumble of contradictions.

Turning away, the man pointed eastward. "Have you ever wondered what happened to it?"

"To what?" Jim asked.

"To the Moon, boy!"

"Everyone wonders that," Jim replied.

"Ahh, not so, my young friend," the old man said, shaking his head as he did. Long strands of white hair fell out of his dark hood. "After a few years out here," he waved his hand at the rock-strewn dunes around them, "most people stop asking questions, and care only about survival. It is the way of Ruin."

The stranger glanced back at Jim and added, "I see in your eyes a curiosity that burns despite this terrible place. The desert is where imagination comes to die."

Turning back toward the horizon, the man continued, "Legend says, our Moon was broken by the gods as punishment for mankind's arrogance. Its ruinous passage was meant to remind us that we, being so much smaller, are that much more fragile."

Jim said nothing, so the man continued, "You see, it is said, we rebelled against the gods. We warred with them, and, as punishment, they destroyed the paradise they had created for us. In the millenia since that great forgotten war, mankind has paid a heavy penance for our arrogance."

Jim continued to watch the broken Moon as it crawled skyward. It illuminated the desert. Long lines of cool light were broken by the shadows of boulders among the sand. Some of the sand on the rocky archway that they had moored the ship to seemed to sparkle in the glow.

Turning back to the old man, he asked, "What penance?"

The stranger strode to Jim's side. Looking out, he swept his hand to the west, "Tell me Jim, what do you see?"

He raised an eyebrow and replied, "I see dunes, rocks, and the broken Moon."

The man grunted as he stretched his hands wider. "To the north, the Eternal Mountains and the Black Forest bar the passage to the plains of The Northern Tribes. To the east, beyond the Great Dune Sea and the unceasing storms, lies a jungle with all new types of dangers. None of your generation have survived the horrors of the desert to reach it, but it's there."

Jim set a questioning glance toward the old man, but said nothing.

"To the south, the Holy Lands burn under a relentless sun, but a great evil rises from the inferno. In the east and deep south, far over the horizon, the salt sea consumes man and metal. Our world is an unforgiving wasteland. It never gives. Only takes. Our world is a perilous place. It was not always this way, but for nearly ten thousand years, mankind has served a steep sentence, whether they realize it or not."

The man straightened a bit as he concluded, "Now, though, the sentence has been served. Our full potential will soon be realized. How lucky you are to see such times!"

Jim stared upward at the twinkling stars. "Great story, but what does—" Jim looked down. The man had vanished. He was talking to himself.

As dreams go, this one is one of the craziest, he thought.

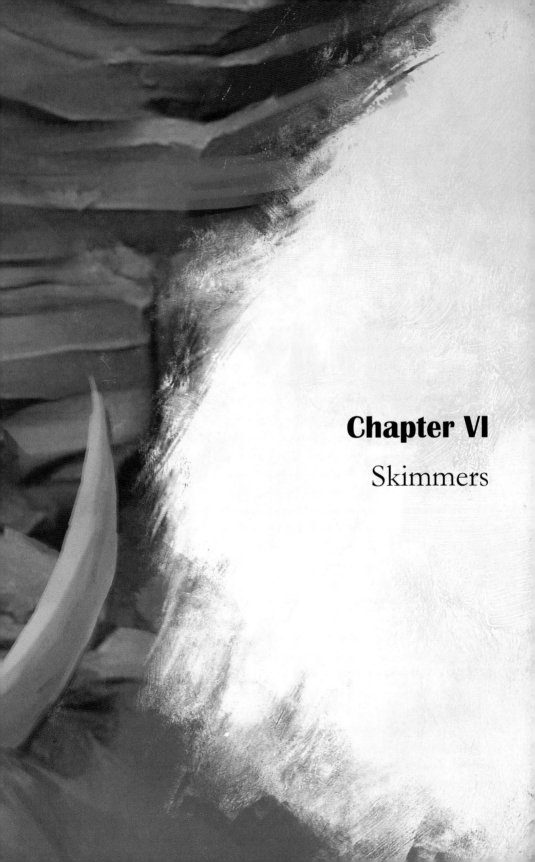

Chapter VI

Skimmers

It was an early start for the group. This far out in the wastes there was very little to slow the onward drive of the morning winds. Trade across the Great Dune Sea was heavily reliant on the morning and early evening winds, also called "Twilight Winds."

Every day, just before the rising of the sun, powerful gusts would blow from the southeast and last until noon. Later, as the last of the day's light faded behind the western reaches, it would again blow, this time from the northwest. The best traders could time their maneuvers perfectly and ride the life-giving winds over two-hundred kilometers a day.

The sloop creaked and protested with each whistling gust, but with Jim at the helm, they were making excellent time. His navigational skills were second-to-none. That, and perhaps his skill with a scimitar. Henry, in his usual chipper mood, said, "You know gents, at this rate, I suspect we'll reach Rock Bottom well before the afternoon calm."

Jim nodded in agreement and then stole a glance at Sasha. The boy's face was downturned and pale. He dragged his feet around the deck as he went about his duties, trying to ignore the constant rocking and the nausea it induced. The wind was blowing especially hard that morning, and it demanded all hands on deck to keep their ship on the shifting dune peaks and not stranded in a ditch.

The best way to travel the wastes was to keep one's ship on the constantly shifting ridgelines, grabbing as much wind as possible while keeping out of the blasting sand bowls between each dune. Out this far, the drops could be hundreds of feet and trap less experienced helmsmen.

Shielding his eyes from another blast of sand, Jim regretted leaving the gunner's goggles back at the Liberator. He glanced at Henry, who had been whistling an eerie tune while retying the halyard, and inquired, "How is it you can move about without sand clogging up your gears?"

Henry finished the tie with a grunt and rolled over until he came to a stop next to Jim. His shade brightened at the opportunity for conversation. He grabbed the wheel with one hand and motioned toward Jim with the other. "Here, place your hand just above my chassis, but do it very slowly," he said.

Henry's hand held the wheel steady with little effort, so Jim let go. Slowly, he moved his hand closer to Henry. Suddenly, it slowed, as if plunging into an invisible wall of… something. Pushing slightly harder, he broke through whatever it was, and touched cold metal. He could feel the gentle hum of Henry's ether cube and the whirring of gears as they steadily turned, some of them visible behind the brass and steel breastplate.

Henry laughed at Jim's confused stare and said, "That's called a repulsor field."

"A what now?"

"Repulsor field," Henry repeated. "Every ether cube has it. It isn't strong enough to stop something like, say, a musket ball or rifled bullet, or even a hastily thrown rock, but it keeps sand and debris from turning me into a Henry statue. The tech is far beyond geartech; made by the ancients."

Sasha plodded his way over to the group, wiping some fresh vomit from the side of his mouth. "You know Henry," he said between hiccups. "my mother always said, find unique friends. I'd say you qualify."

"I say, lad," Henry said as his metallic eyebrows furrowed and his irises constricted, "You look dreadful. I'd have thought you'd have taken to the motion of suspended travel by now. You took to the Liberator with ease."

Sasha burped. His hand covered his mouth as he held back another urge to vomit. After a moment of recovery, he replied, "Yeah well, the Liberator is like a giant steady swing. Riding in this thing though," he stomped on the slatted deck, "is like being rolled down a hill in a barrel."

From the east, warmth heralded the arrival of another day. Rays of light spread skyward. As the sun breached the horizon, a new gust of wind pushed Jim into the wheel, and Sasha to the railing.

After another bout of retching, Sasha returned to the group. "So, Rock Bottom!" he exclaimed, having recovered for a moment, "You know, I've always wanted to see it. I hear it's a pretty wild place."

Jim nodded, "Yeah, you could say that. Chaotic is how I'd put it. Just keep your money close when we get there. Pickpockets are..." He paused and tilted his head.

Henry asked curiously, "Are what? Jim?"

"Shh. Do you hear that?" Jim squinted his eyes and scanned the horizon. A faint droning grew, riding upon the wind. "It's not coming from the direction of Rock Bottom."

Sasha tilted his head too, "Wait a sec. Yeah. I think I hear it. It sounds like... buzzing. Maybe insects?"

Henry shook his metallic head, "No. The nearest body of water is the river at Freeport. That's a week away from here. The supply at Rock Bottom is a series of deep wells so... I... I recognize that sound. Like fabric in a stiff breeze."

The buzzing was still faint but had begun to pierce even the roaring winds. "Look!" Sasha pointed to the northeast. "See that? Something's coming over the dunes. Jim. Are those sails?"

Jim strained his eyes. After a few moments, he spotted them. Indeed, small figures, too small to be ships, were approaching from the north, moving swiftly across the sand. He could barely make out the tiny triangular sails in the distance.

Seconds crawled by painfully as the silhouettes grew closer. Now, Jim really wished he had brass goggles with a distance lens attached. Next to him, Henry's mechanical irises buzzed and whirred as he stared at the small white dots. Suddenly, Henry cried, "Bloody hell! Those aren't ships. They're Skimmers."

Jim's blood went cold. Through the sand and heat haze, he could make out small, stick-like figures clinging to masts only slightly taller than themselves. He'd seen these types of craft before, unfortunately. Pulling his scimitar from its scabbard, he shouted over the wind, "Cannibals! It's gonna get ugly!"

The tiny craft, favored by cannibals, were hardly two meters long and just as tall. They consisted of an oval-shaped pushstone base, a raw Manzawood mast, and framed sail.

The rider held onto a crude bar protruding from each end of the frame, and leaning back, "skimmed" along at the mercy of the wind, hovering just above the ground. It was a dangerous mode of transportation for the common man, but perfect for thrill seekers, racers, and of course, half-crazed cannibals.

Panic crept into Sasha's voice. "What the hell are they doing this far east? I count at least... two dozen of them."

Henry chuckled. It was deep and strange in his metallic throat. An icy glee was in his voice, "That's right. Terrible odds for them, so don't go killing the lot before I get my chance."

He rolled over to the starboard swivel gun. The weapon's brass body was nearly unrecognizable under a layer of patina. Henry unplugged the barrel and shoved a gunpowder charge in. He followed it with a measured handful of grapeshot.

Jim could hear the chants of the cannibals carrying over their droning craft now. Streamers fluttered over the top of each skimmer with a loud buzzing. Multiplied twenty times over, the sound was loud and more than a little intimidating.

The first of the cannibals sailed close enough to be heard over the buzzing streamers. He was mostly naked aside from a tattered loincloth. His shoulders, knees, and elbows were covered in bone armor. Most disturbing, though, was his helmet. Through the sand, Jim could see that it had been fashioned from a human skull. Its teeth had been sharpened and the skull painted with unknown symbols.

With a deep, gravelly voice, the leader shouted at the group, "Chok no gah!" Detaching a spear from his mast, he held it above his head and chanted louder, "Chok no gah!" Soon, the rest of the cannibals followed, chanting the phrase over and over.

Jim gripped his scimitar tighter and muttered, "Guns would be a big help right about now."

The attackers drew closer to the ship and Henry zeroed in on the leader. As he crouched behind the swivel cannon, he shouted over the wind, "With the ship rocking about as it is, rifles wouldn't do much good." He patted the brass cannon. "This little beauty though, with the amount of metal she's about to spew, ha, she'd knock the arse off a fly at fifty yards."

Jim started the count in his head.

Thirty meters.

"Just a bit closer boys," Henry sighted in the swivel gun. "Sure, I could hit you from here, but we're going for maximum fear factor."

Wakes of sand erupted from the skimmers as they bobbed up and down, sometimes striking the dunetops.

Twenty meters.

Shouting and buzzing filled the air. Hungry cannibals continued to yell, "Chok no gah!" With each meter, their chanting grew louder.

Ten meters.

"Smile and wait for the flash!" Henry's voice was darkening.

Jim gripped his scimitar tightly and braced against the railing. "You know, Henry," he called, his voice shaking, "Maybe you should take this a bit more ser-"

BOOM.

Henry's swivel cannon exploded in a cloud of choking black smoke. His metal body was thrown backwards as the breach blasted open from its rusted clasps. He rolled sideways along the deck and struck the port railing with a metallic *clang*. He lay motionless, face blackened from the backfire.

"Dammit!" Jim shouted.

A shrill scream broke from the nearest cannibal. Despite the ruination of their sole swivel cannon, the grapeshot had escaped with enough velocity to do its mortal deed. Blood sprayed the sand as the leader tumbled backwards.

The next skimmer struck the ship with a loud *thud*. Catapulting himself over the railing, a cannibal met the cold steel of Sasha's scimitar. The boy's eyes were wide with horror as he watched the deadly effect of his blow.

Jim shouted in alarm, "Sasha, behind you!"

Two more cannibals had boarded the ship from aft and were charging from behind the shocked boy. These were less armored than their leader, being clad in shoulder and shin armor only. One of them wore a bandage across his left eye. No doubt a wound from some previous victim who had been unwilling to go without a fight. He growled through sharpened teeth as he charged with his comrade.

Jim arrived at Sasha's side, just in time to bat away the first spear with his sword.

Jim threw his weight into the starving creature and shot his weapon out sideways to slash open the second cannibal on the way down. While he rolled across the deck, grappling with the enemy, Sasha pierced the second cannibal through the chest. The man collapsed to his knees, clutching at the wound, trying in vain to stem the tide of death.

Jim quickly gained the upper hand against the other cannibal who was two heads smaller than himself. A solid right cross sent the man's skull into the wooden deck planks. Quickly, jumping to his feet, Jim tossed the limp body over the railing and onto the sand with a *thud*.

New shouts erupted from all around the ship. The rest of the raiders had surrounded their small sloop and were scaling the railings on three sides. Stealing a few breaths, Jim glanced at Sasha. The boy's face was ghost white as he stared off somewhere beyond the waking world.

Jim trotted over and set his hand on Sasha's shoulder, snapping the boy from his trance. He spoke as calmly as he could between heavy breaths, "Try not to think about it. There'll be plenty of time for that afterwards."

Without a pilot at the wheel, the ship bucked and listed violently. Sprays of sand poured over the deck, mixing with the blood of fallen cannibals. More hungry figures poured over the railing. "We aren't going to win this one, are we?" Sasha asked.

Jim considered lying to the boy. "No," he finally said. "Probably not."

Sasha's voice was shaking, "Do you think you can pull another trick like you did back on the Liberator?"

Jim shook his head, "No. I'll more likely destroy our ship by accident, and to be honest, I don't even know how to summon them or use them, or whatever you call it. It's like the sands choose me, not the other way around. How about you?"

Sasha's eyes shot left and right. Frustrated, he replied, "No fire to work off of. Henry had the matches for the swivel gun. Besides, I'm barely at an acolyte level. I'd burn out before we got through half these guys."

Their inundated vessel sagged backwards, its rudder sending hissing sprays of sand as cannibals piled on.

Jim could hear Sasha's unsteady breathing. The young man was terrified. If Jim was honest with himself, he wasn't doing much better.

"This sucks," Sasha said as the last cannibal cleared the railing.

"Yeah," Jim replied. "Sucks bad." The leather on his scimitar's hilt creaked and his knuckles went white. With his free hand, he pointed and said, "They have at least an extra meter's reach with those spears. When they charge, try to duck and roll into their legs. They lose their advantage at a short distance. I'll take the right group, you take the left."

"What? And leave me the scraps?"

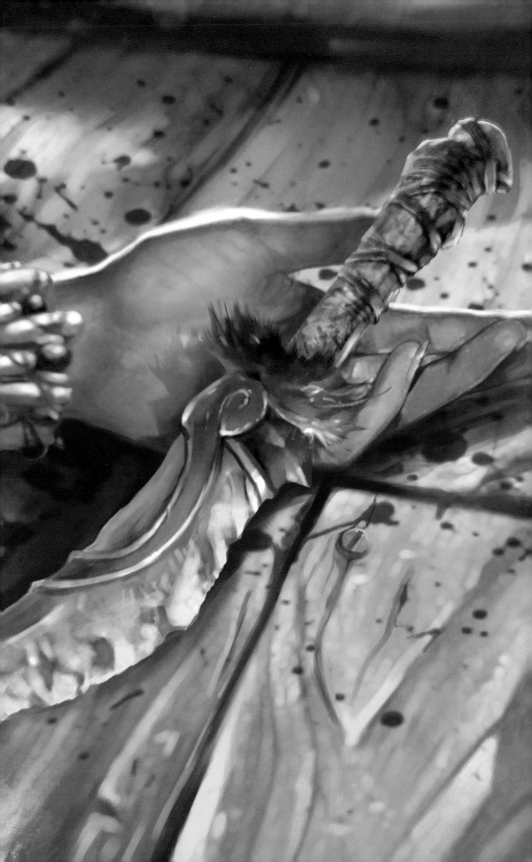

Suddenly, a figure whirred by them toward the aft deck. It was Henry. In his hand was the destroyed swivel cannon, still dangling from its mount. He'd ripped the entire emplacement straight from the railing. Its muzzle had been splayed outward and blackened.

Wielding the small cannon like a meat tenderizer, Henry let loose a frightening metallic war cry as he descended on the first group. The cannibals hesitated, which was enough to be their undoing.

The clockwork man spun impossibly fast, striking down anyone in range of his bludgeon. Heads, arms, torsos, nothing was spared. Blood soon sloshed across the deck with each howling gust of wind. In seconds, Henry had cut a dozen down in a frenzy.

One man attempted to dive over the railing, but his legs were severed in mid-air. He screamed as his body cartwheeled to a sand ridge below. For a moment, Jim caught a look in Henry's eyes. Despite their artificial glow, he could see it as clear as if he'd been looking into the eyes of a man. Henry was out of his mind.

Jim would sort that out later. There was a fight to be finished. He and Sasha shouted, invigorated by their shift of fortune, charging into the fray. They closed with a group of five very frightened, very surprised cannibals.

Steel met flesh and bone. Screams and shouts filled the air as more men were felled.

For a few moments, the melee was complete chaos. Braver, or perhaps foolish foes attempted to disable Henry by tossing their spears at the spinning clockwork man, but they were simply deflected off his pirouetting chassis. Henry continued his attack, laughing maniacally as he culled the cannibals.

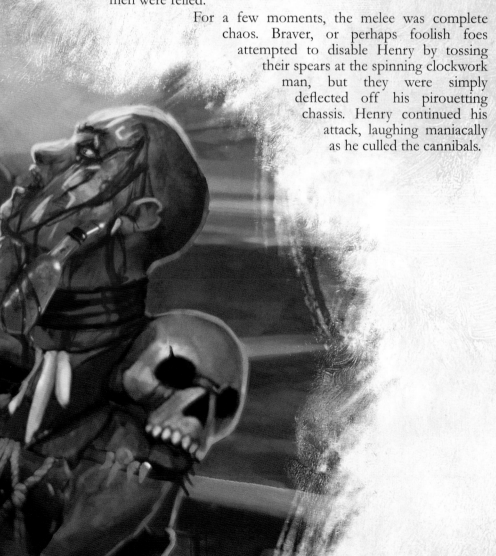

Amidst the confusion, a cannibal pinned Sasha to the deck. Both had lost their weapons in the struggle, and the man's hands were around the boy's throat. Jim had his own problems as he attempted to fend off the attacks of two very determined cannibals.

Contorting sideways, Jim expertly swatted both spears away and closed range. The nearest cannibal dropped his weapon and attempted to grab Jim by his sword arm. For his efforts, one of the man's arms was swiftly severed from his body.

From the corner of his eye, Jim caught sight of Sasha attempting to reach something from his boot. The boy's face was turning blue. Suddenly, in a quick motion, Sasha unsheathed a hunting knife from its hiding spot and plunged it into his attacker's neck. The cannibal, wide-eyed with grim surprise, opened his mouth to scream, but his windpipe was blocked by the steel blade.

As Sasha withdrew the blade, blood sprayed the deck and himself. Screaming, he continued to plunge it over and over into the flailing body of the dying cannibal.

Slicing upwards, Jim cut the last attacker from stomach to neck. He thrust again with the tipped end of his sharpened blade, pushing it until it emerged out of the man's back. The cannibal stared ahead with dull eyes for a moment. Following a sloppy wet cough of blood, his eyes rolled back in his head and he slumped against the railing.

The remnants of the raiders regrouped at the aft deck. Taking a quick break from his wanton destruction, Henry rolled to a stop next to his winded counterparts. He slapped Sasha on the back.

Speaking loud enough for the half-terrified cannibals to hear, he remarked, "Well, my boy. It looks like there's only a handful of them left. Would you like to do the honors or shall I?"

Sasha, crestfallen and covered in blood, dry heaved. Jim scowled at Henry. "He's never killed before. It's not easy… the first time."

Henry spoke, slightly subdued by Jim's words, "Ah… Sorry lad. I didn't know. You two sit back and enjoy the show. I'll take care of this lot."

In a blur, Henry dashed toward the frightened group of cannibals. Despair was written on their faces as their doom approached. Again, he was a tornado of death. His spinning form struck a cannibal who had not been quick enough to jump overboard. Two more men disappeared into a mist of red mid-jump.

The rest of the group had already decided to conform to the age old adage, "Discretion is the better part of valor," and in full panic, jumped for their lives to the sand below. In short order, their Skimmers retreated into the distance, wakes of sand following their frightened escape.

Turning to the pair, Henry was glowing a deep shade of purple instead of his usual blue. He glanced around the blood-covered deck. "Well," he said, tossing the spent swivel gun aside like matchwood, "you picked a hell of a day to be on deck cleaning duty, eh Sasha?"

The boy collapsed.

Much of the rest of the afternoon was spent cleaning up the bloody main deck. Henry's rampage left a complete mess of body parts and blood. He'd opted to help Jim with the cleanup while Sasha spent time below deck, recovering from his ordeal.

Hours passed without a word said as man and machine toiled. Tossing the last limb overboard, Jim finally pulled Henry aside. "You mind explaining what happened earlier?" he asked..

Henry's usual bright tone dimmed slightly, "I… I'm sorry, Jim. I guess, in the heat of battle, I just lost it. I don't know why. Sometimes, in the thick of battle, it happens. I lose my faculties." Henry's glow darkened a little more.

He nodded and asked, "Does your ether cube change colors depending on your mood?"

Henry looked down at his glowing midsection, "Ah, sorry about that. The captain made the same observation in our last raid. She and I are both at a loss for why it happened. As far as I know, ether cubes don't change color. My mood is reflected in the level of light I give off, not its hue."

A *clop clop clop* sound echoed from the hold as Sasha slowly ascended the stairs, still white with sickness. At the carnage, the rocking of the ship, or perhaps both, Jim wasn't sure.

He spoke quietly, "Hey guys. I, uhh… Should we use some of the water reserves to clean up the blood? Some of it, umm, is leaking below deck."

Jim glanced at Henry. For once, he was keeping quiet. Sighing, Jim shrugged, "Water should never be wasted. We can leave it to the port laborers."

The sun was still hanging in the eastern horizon, at least an hour from noon. Its glow fired the sand in a trail of burning reds and oranges. The fight had felt like hours but in reality, it had been a few minutes.

Through the heat haze, Jim spotted what could only be the clock tower of Rock Bottom. He glanced at Sasha whose shirt was caked in dark dry blood. "Perhaps," he said, as gently as he could, "you should have a change of clothes before we head into town."

Chapter VII
Rock Bottom

Rock Bottom was a city full of contradictions. Occupying a space between two great cultures does that to a place. Even from a distance, the skyline of the city of fifty thousand, give or take ten thousand in the winter and summer, was a mix of regal stone architecture of the northern protectorate and the more practical mud brick dwellings found among Alliance towns.

As their sloop pulled into port, the beautiful clock tower, twenty stories high and located in the cultural and literal center of the city, announced it was 1PM. The loud gong echoed down the webworks of winding streets and the stone faces of buildings. One could even hear the loud clang as the metal gear-catch behind the clock face dropped into a new slot.

The greyed stone spire stood out; an immovable beacon of civilization against a bleary and unforgiving desert. Around it, all manner of buildings had sprung up. The entire city seemed to rise upward toward the clock tower.

The blood plastered sloop creaked to a stop as Jim furled the sail and Henry weighed anchor. A soft *thump* reverberated through the wooden hull as Sasha turned the wheel and slid the ship sideways into the dock pylons. Two workers wearing head-to-toe white garb, a necessity in protecting oneself during daily work in the unforgiving sun, grabbed the lines thrown to them and secured the small vessel to the dock.

Jim and Sasha made their way down the ship's bowing gangway. Covertly passing a generous handful of black coins to each man, Jim whispered, "Had a run in with some cannibals. My friend and I left a bit of a mess. Discreet cleaning, please." The workers stared wide eyed at the crimson stained deck behind him.

"I'll say," the larger of the two men replied. He opened a latched storage crate near the bottom of the gangway and withdrew a hand-pumped pressure washer. The device was made of two cylinders attached to a ratcheting strap that met a pair of shoulder harnesses. One cylinder was marked "WATER" and the other "GRIT."

"Will it be the full treatment, or the poor man's scrub?" the worker asked.

"The scrub," Jim replied.

"Water and grit it is," the man said, and marched up the gangplank.

Seeing the wary glances of the other worker, Sasha stepped forward and dropped a few more coins into his eager hands. "And we'd appreciate it if you two kept out of the hold. We have goods for trade that we'd rather avoid disturbing."

Henry had reluctantly agreed to stay below deck. Even in the far reaches, the Prophetess had eyes, and illegal clockwork tech would draw far too much attention.

The first man, who had already begun pumping the deck wash backpack, called down, "I'm afraid the Rock Bottom Port Authority requires that we search the holds of all incoming ships for contraband and ensure their contents are both legal and safe. In accordance with paragraph-"

"Perhaps these coins should go to the port authority then. Though I can't promise the money will be properly distributed to the workers tasked with cleanup," Jim interrupted.

"No need," the closer of the two workers replied with a smile. "She'll be cleaned and unmolested. You can count on it."

Jim caught the man in an intense stare until he was sure the fellow was genuine. Finally, he nodded and started toward the dockmaster's office.

"Not bad, boss," Sasha commented as they walked across the decaying dock and onto a connecting stone pathway. "You have a gift for intimidating folks."

Jim shook his head. "Don't call me boss, and out here bribing is practically a virtue, right up there with cleanliness."

Sasha laughed. Already, his color was returning. Every step further from the sloop seemed to bring back his good cheer. They rounded another corner. The street began to incline as they headed in the direction of the town center. Around them, the sand was slowly thinning out, revealing a proper cobblestone street.

"So, Jim," Sasha said, "After the dockmaster, where to?"

"A barber," Jim replied. "If I have to spend another day looking at that hair of yours..."

As they ventured deeper, the city grew more and more densely packed. Soon, the space from one building to another was so small, the walls just seemed to melt together, their stones crooked and crushed in some places. Pipes and drains snaked down every surface, some ending in gutter drains and others disappearing into the cobblestone sidewalk. They gurgled and groaned as dishes clanging, voices, and any manner of domestic life spilled out from the insides of the buildings.

Finally, they reached the market sector.

Cigar smoke, mixed with the smell of burning manzawood and garlic, added to the frenetic procession that was Main Street Market.

A massive wooden sign, at least twenty meters wide and nearly as tall, sat atop a rusted pole at the center of the marketplace. Down the middle was drawn a line in white.

    To the left, the words "WASTE NOT" were painted with an arrow next to them. To the right, "WANT NOT" with a similar arrow pointing right.

    On the left side of the market, vendors peddled every type of desert spice, food items, water, and other consumables of survival. At some stands, edible insects, and plants from every corner of Ruin were on display. Jim spotted a stand selling hundreds of steamed scorpions, with the poisonous gland and stinger removed. Each hung from a small line of twine.

    For those who could afford it, fruits, berries, and even auroch meat adorned the tables of some of the more luxurious vendors. Next to them, hired guards, little more than local thugs, stood watch, weapons in hand, ready to dissuade any would-be thief.

To the right, in the "WANT NOT" section, weapons vendors peddled poorly cared for muskets, scimitars, and other tools of war. These stands were guarded by hired hands. Most wielded axes, swords, and other sharpened weapons, with the wealthier vendors hiring guards with six shooter pistols. Judging by the looks on their faces, little was left to the imagination on what they would do to anyone stupid enough to steal from their clients.

One woman's cart was loaded to tipping with springs, gears, cogs, and screws. Jim thought he might have spotted the familiar blue glow of an ether crystal. A rare find at any market, and technically illegal, not that any of the city guards would arrest her for such a crime. In fact, the city had very few guards. Those who could afford protection would pay for it, and those who couldn't had better be handy with a weapon.

Men on unwieldy bicycles with enormous front wheels wobbled their way down the middle of the street. Meanwhile, children ran underfoot, invested in whatever imaginary adventure they fancied for the day. They squealed and giggled as they played.

Overhead, some of the more privileged upper class pedaled by on zip balloons, their boredom of affluent life quite obvious in their dull faces. The small three-meter long contraptions they rode were nothing more than miniature burners feeding a steady supply of black crystal steam into a balloon, and suspending a propeller-driven bicycle from small steel straps. The rudder and propellers would turn together as the rider turned the handles. It was a terrible waste of precious water and black crystal in Jim's opinion.

Jim and Sasha pushed through the mass of humanity and made their way to a nearby barbershop. The entrance was almost overrun with vendor carts on the "WANT NOT" side. The owner, balding and sporting a well-waxed twisted mustache, shouted at a pair of cart owners. They crowded the front of his shop, calling out, attempting to sell clocks, or some other sort of complicated device. Jim couldn't quite tell.

As he and Sasha approached the entrance, they spotted four men in vertical striped suits singing in tight harmony next to the shop. The song was a mix of the controlled, Grand Vocal music of the Protectorate performance halls and the wild conflagration of 'Izalatan peasant diddys.

The pair stopped and watched the men sing for a minute.

In the good ol' summertime. When the skies were blue.
You held your hand in mine, and you said you'd always be true.
But those days have come and gone, and you've left me standing here.
Now I look to the sky with eyes that cry and...

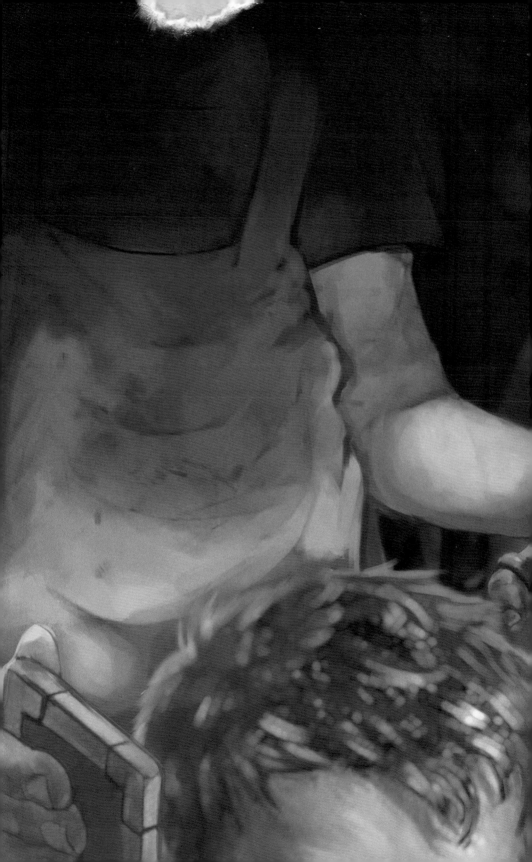

Finally, squeezing by the last obstacle, and dropping a few coins in the hat of one of the singers, Jim and Sasha made their way inside. The door shut behind them, and instantly the bedlam of the outside world was dulled. Jim let out a deep sigh. "Now you see why I avoid cities like a plague."

Sasha was beaming. "Are you kidding me!? That was great! The streets of Togsov were dark, dirty, and outright scary sometimes. Here? This place is alive!"

Jim just shook his head. "I'll take my ship and the sand any day." He tried to shake the ringing out of his ears from all the commotion.

Just then, the bell above the door jingled as the plump mustached owner squeezed through backward, still shouting at the men outside, "Gods curse you fools! I hope your stupid trinkets rust, moronic imbecels!" The door slammed behind him as he huffed and puffed his considerable mass across the barbershop floor. "Ugh, they'll be out of business in a week anyhow," he muttered.

"Damn vultures! Selling their garbage is no pain to them, but how am I, a legitimate businessman, supposed to stay in business with the likes of them clogging up my shopfront?"

After taking a breath, he spotted the pair and painted on a well practiced smile, "Ah! Jim, my good man. It has been quite some time." The man offered him a strong handshake. "What brings you back to Rock B— GODS ABOVE BOY. What in blazes have you done to your hair?"

Jim laughed.

Seeing the red tint crossing Sasha's face, He cleared his throat. "Cherum, this is Sasha. Sasha, Cherum."

The man beamed a smile as he shook the boy's hand. "Sorry lad. I meant no offense. I can only assume you've come here to correct that…"

Sasha nodded and groaned.

Cherum made his way to a worn barber chair and gestured. "Please, sit."

The priest smelled it. Faint in the air, the unique call of an Awakened, *no… two of them. One carries a much stronger presence than the other. Hmmm.*

He closed his eyes to focus his second sight. Rock Bottom was teaming with life, but he was searching for two very unique individuals among thousands of inconsequential animals.

Walking slowly, with eyes closed, he was careful to keep his hood drawn up. Not an easy undertaking in the sweltering heat of late day. Rock Bottom was a free port and agents of the Prophetess, agents like him, were outlawed here.

The man mused as he searched, *Let them try and stop us. The time is so near now. These empty creatures will soon consider themselves lucky to live in the time of rebirth. Praise be to her —* "OOF."

The man was suddenly knocked off balance by a food cart in his path. Some of the fruit rolled onto the ground with a *plop plop*. A mercenary guard shuffled his overweight body into the priest's path. He stank of sweat and sex. Where he spent his daily wages was painfully apparent.

Pushing his way past the towering guard, the cart's owner pointed a sun-weathered finger at him, "Watch it, you old fool!" he shouted "Are you blind or just a moron? I'm trying to conduct business here, and people like you— HEY! I'm talking to you! "

The man's voice faded into the background as the disguised priest pushed further into the crowd. He was on the hunt now and cared only for the location of his quarry. To him, Unawakened were just empty specimens of humanity. Meaningless things. Not worth his time or attention. He continued on.

Gradually, the distinct sound of two Awakened individuals rose above the chaos. *There! I can smell them. Oh! By her name, there is an Awakened of earth among them! To capture one of those… my reward will be significant,* he thought, his glee hurrying his gait with new life.

Ahead of him, the sign of a barber hung above a store building with its curtains drawn shut.

In quick order, the skillful craftsman had transformed Sasha's bowl cut to something resembling the socially acceptable "slick wave," a heavily gelled sideways comb, typical among the middle class of northern cities. Satisfied with his work, Cherum turned back to Jim, who was half dozing in a waiting chair.

"Well, to nobody's surprise, I'm a miracle worker," Cherum stated proudly.

Jim sat up and smirked. "If you do say so yourself," he replied.

"Damn right, Jimmy. However, I doubt you navigated the wastes and floated into town just to get your young friend a haircut." He turned to Sasha and added, "No offense lad, but I've known Jim for quite a few years, and friends aren't something he handles well, or at all."

Sasha was still examining his new look in the wall mirror and smiling, "Sir, after fixing the mess on my head, you'd have to make a serious effort to offend me."

The good-humored barber laughed heartily and turned to Jim. "So, now that business is handled, let's get down to more business."

Cherum sat in one of his barber chairs. The leathered cushions creaked and sighed under his considerable girth. Suddenly, a silver bowl-shaped device, which had been affixed to the back of the chair, fell forward with a loud CLANG atop Cherum's head.

"These damned things!" he lamented as he stood up and wrestled with the device, which was now belching steam and smoke. "Serves me right for buying into a gimmick. 'It will be well worth the investment,' they said. 'Oh yes, it can straighten hair in mere minutes,' they said. Well, sure, if it doesn't burn my place down first, I -"

Jim cleared his throat.

"Ahh right, the business," Cherum said, finally disconnecting a metal tube from the chair. It sighed another puff of smoke and fell silent. He sat down again and continued, "I assume you need something. You aren't the type for social calls after all. So what can this humble barber do for you today, my strong silent friend?"

Jim leaned forward and replied quietly, "I need to make a trade in a sizeable amount of black. Can you line someone up for us? There's a ten percent finder's fee in it if you do."

Cherum's wide smile turned mischievous. "Ahh! So it's *that* kind of business? Let's make this meeting a bit more private then, shall we?" He got up from his chair with a grunt and walked across the room. There was a loud *BANG* as he struck a metal-plated box attached to the wall above the windows. Two blackout curtains from hidden dropout panels fell into place.

The sound of the outside world was further muffled, to Jim's great relief. Cherum locked the door and made his way back over to the table. Jim overheard him mumbling, "It's not like I'll attract any customers with those vermin gracing my doorstep anyhow."

Finally, satisfied with his security precautions, Cherum dragged a foldable chair into the waiting area. Motioning for Sasha to join them, he leaned back, his potbelly nearly bursting through his unwashed, grease stained work shirt.

"So, ten percent eh? Jim, you devil! You know my fee is fifteen. Don't mistake my kind demeanor with charity. I've never heard of the word." Jim stole a sly grin at Sasha, who was watching the exchange with some interest.

"But, doesn't your name mean charity in the old tongue?" Jim asked.

"The old tongue. Take note, Jimmy," Cherum replied. "Ahh, that reminds me, that'll be six bits for the boy's haircut. Miracles aren't cheap, you know."

Jim feigned deep thought as he stroked his chin. Finally, feeling that he had led the man on long enough, he leaned in. "Very well, fifteen percent it is. And here's your coin." Handing Cherum his payment, Jim pressed the money between their palms and shook his hand.

Shaking a person's hand as means of depositing money into it was common practice in most trading cities of Ruin. It was considered a sign of trust between buyer and seller. It also worked quite well at hiding the true sum of money for the purpose of bribes and tips, not that either was distinguishable from the other in Rock Bottom. In his case, Jim slipped two more bits in as a "thank you."

The deal done, Jim lowered his voice. "We need to get our hands on about ten thousand kilos of unrefined black crystal. We need it by early morning tomorrow too."

Cherum whistled in amazement. "By the gods, Jimmy. Ten thousand? What in the cannie-tainted wastes do you need that much for? You could steam lift a damn building for a month with that much black. Also, since when did you work with… well, anyone?", he asked, glancing at Sasha before adding, "You've been a loner ever since you first wandered in here, oh… what has it been? Ten years now, I suppose."

"Sasha here is an… apprentice business partner," Jim responded. "And you know better than to ask. As for the quantity, I just need to know if it's possible, otherwise, we can easily search out another finder." He spotted an enthusiastic grin on Sasha's face.

Jim had performed this dance with Cherum and countless other black market dealers for years. Antisocial or not, it was a skill Jim, and any competent trader had to know. The dealer would first inflate the value of their business prowess. The trader, Jim in this case, would threaten to find another buyer, and finally, the dealer would decide "grudgingly" to work with him.

It was Cherum's move. The half barber, half black market dealer waved away Jim's suggestion. "No no no, I can find you a supplier, Jimmy. I just get curious, is all. Being cooped up in this place all day gets a bit boring."

Jim nodded. Sasha sat quietly by, content to soak in all he could as he watched with wide eyes while the two men practiced their trades.

Cherum lowered his voice again. Jim and Sasha leaned in as the barber spoke, "Okay, tonight, midnight at the Blue Belly Saloon. Your guy will be there. Wait at the table next to the piano."

Seeing Jim's frown, Cherum added, "Sorry, Jimmy. I know how you despise the throngs of humanity, but the loud music makes business conversation much easier. As it says in the Poesies of the Night Prince-"

He cleared his throat and his eyes looked skyward in practiced ritual.

"'Twere night. 'Twere silent.
'Twere ears all around.
'Twas not the time.
'Twas not the place.
Fere dealings underground."

Jim leaned forward to finish Cherum's poem.

"Were there crowds or music.
Were there heaviest of rain.
I would deal the night most darkly.
And fear not the lawman's spane."

"Ha!" Cherum exclaimed, "I see the desert sun hasn't dulled your memory, Jimmy. You even used proper speech in the second half of the poem." He nodded to Sasha, "Just as was custom in all of the Night Prince's pieces."

"Excuse me," Sasha asked, "but, who is the Night Prince and what's a spane?"

Cherum, seeing a fresh young mind to influence, happily replied, "Ahh! The Poems of the Night Prince are a cherished work among those who deal erm… in the shadows. I suggest you find a copy, post-haste. He is believed to be the founder of the Guild of Black Cloaks. A bit of a legend around here, seeing as how he was born here in Rock Bottom, three thousand and some odd years ago. This place was little more than an outpost in those days."

"And the spane?" Sasha asked.

"The spane was a sort of truncheon used at the time the book was written, somewhere around the year A.F. 6400. It was popular among the guards of the ancient cities. They built it from strips of suahim leather tightened into a bundle around a bag of quicklime powder at the end," Cherum replied.

He turned his right fist in his left hand. "You see, the lawmen would turn the handle clockwise to tighten the leather around the lime. It would click into place by increments. The tighter the turn, the harder you had to hit someone to release the lime. When an unfortunate lawbreaker was struck with it, the leather would loosen just enough to release bits of the powder. The solution mixes with sweat and causes severe burns. You wouldn't want to be the person on the receiving end of such a tool." Cherum shivered.

"That sounds horrible," Sasha said, curling his lips in disgust.

"It was," Cherum said, "And it burned worse and worse with each strike. In some rare cases, a good flogging with a spane could kill a person. The lesson of the poem is — Common criminals deal in dark alleys. Smart ones deal in large crowds."

Jim shrugged, "Well then, tell your man we'll be there. I'll try to spare Sasha the lawman's spane."

Priest Holar. What have you found?

Far north though he was, Her voice was powerful in the priest's mind. He swayed as he stumbled to a dark alleyway to speak to his Prophetess away from the public's gaze. Quickly locating an empty nook between two buildings, he slipped between the structures.

"Your Grace, I have located two Awakened here in Rock Bottom. One of them is likely a former acolyte. His powers are weak but show signs of our instruction. The other is an Awakened of earth, and a feral one at that!"

A sudden wave of nausea overcame him as the Prophetess' voice boomed through his mind.

What? Is it the escapee?

"No, Your Grace. This is a new one. His power is incredible. Certainly the most powerful I have ever seen... apart from yours, your Grace."

The priest could feel her desire, even from so far away.

A rarity worth preserving. Take them alive.

"Your will be done, my Prophetess."

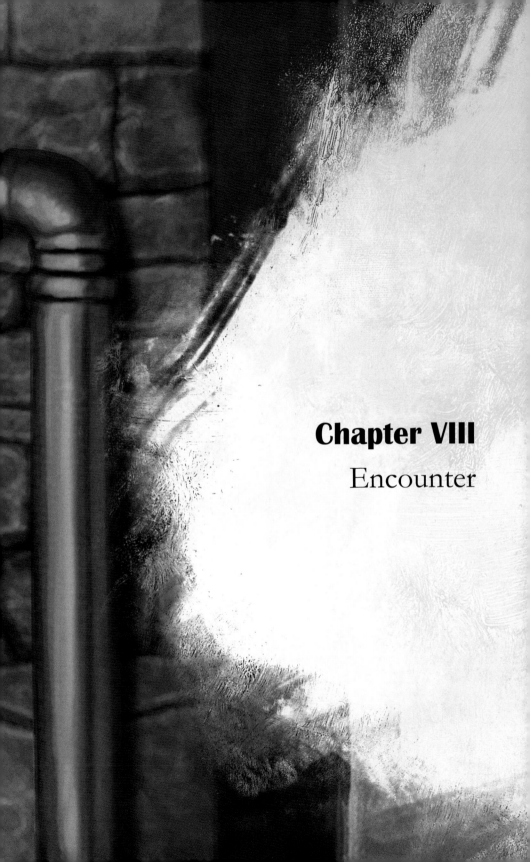

Chapter VIII

Encounter

Raucous music filled the Blue Belly Saloon. Jim and Sasha had indeed been expected: their table in the corner next to the piano was empty and was quite clearly reserved. In a crowded saloon such as this, it stood out like an island in an endless ocean.

Not too subtle, Cherum, Jim thought as he made his way anxiously through the crowd. *Maybe you should have another read-through of your poetry book.*

The two of them pushed through a shoulder-to-shoulder sea of humanity. Most had gathered around the bar to watch the daily Battle of Champions — two contenders attempting to drink each other under the table. This evening's combatants were an odd pair.

One, a hairy man of enormous size and weight, probably a mercenary, swayed as he struggled to find his stein of spiced beer. The other, a much smaller, wild eyed woman with fiery red hair, threw back another gulp with little effort — each time eliciting renewed cheers from the crowd.

At one table, a group of men and women were playing "hoprock." The Game involved thumb-sized pushstone pebbles levitating a few centimeters above the table and a larger fist-sized stone at the far end. The players would press their small pebbles against the table and then let go. Acting against the nearby object, the pebble would launch upward and outward toward the larger pushstone.

The objective was to knock the large stone off the table without losing one's own smaller pebble off the side. The winner would have their drinks paid off for the rest of the night. It was a game that required finesse and concentration. Judging by the red faces and bleary eyes of the players around it, Jim suspected neither was present in particularly great quanities.

A very poorly taxidermied, giant bluebelly lizard protruded from the wall above the bar, its face twisted into what the taxidermist must have convinced himself was a snarl. To Jim, it looked more like a cross-eyed comic character from the paper. He glanced at Sasha, who was laughing and pointing, having reached the same conclusion.

Finally, pushing past the last of the onlookers, they squeezed into their booth. A loud thud from the bar announced the large man had soundly lost the drinking contest. For a moment, the crowd's cheers overwhelmed the piano music. The veteran pianist played on without missing a beat.

Jim sighed and leaned back against the uncomfortable wooden booth seat. It was all too noisy and too crowded. Sasha on the other hand was beaming. "I like this place, Jim. And that lizard. Oh man. I'm dying!"

Jim rolled his eyes. "It's too noisy. How can a man think?"

Sasha clapped his hands somewhat off beat to the wild tune. "Oh come on, Jim. You and I both know, saloons aren't for thinking. They're for drinking!"

A waitress arrived and placed two tall steins of beer on the table. To drive the point home, Sasha threw back a gulp. Some of it missed and spilled down his shirt. He laughed and shrugged.

Jim frowned. "Well, hard as it may be," he warned, "try not to draw too much attention to yourself."

Sasha finished the beer and followed it with a wet burp. He immediately regretted it. Spiced beer was powerful and burned all the way down. In Sasha's case, all the way back up.

Despite his unease, Jim laughed at his sputtering friend. "I'll leave the drinking to you. It's obvious you're the professional here."

Sasha glared at him for a moment. After cleaning himself up and apologizing to the waitress, by way of a coin placed in her hand, he sat down for a slower attempt in round two.

It didn't take long for their contact to show up. The man was ugly and built like a steel press. He reminded Jim of the Liberator's lead deckhand, Harol, though taller. As the man pushed himself onto the bench, he held out a dirt covered hand. Jim reluctantly took it.

The man squeezed and Jim's face twisted into a grimace. *He and Harol should have a contest. I wonder who could press a diamond out of coal the fastest,* he thought as he rubbed the numbness out of his hand.

The stranger began, "Name's Joe. I hear you're lookin' for some black."

"Hey!" Sasha laughed, "Jim, Joe, Joe, Jim! Maybe I should change my name to Jon."

The two men glared at Sasha who cleared his throat nervously and promptly returned to his drink. Jim turned back to Joe and replied, "Yeah. One thousand kilos."

Joe whistled in mock surprise. Jim was sure Cherum had already shared the details of their request but, he had to play the game of trade.

Leaning back, Joe locked his grimy fingers behind his head and feigned deep thought. After an uncomfortable moment of silence, he responded, "I can get you a thousand kilos but, that's a serious haul. My usual clientele are typically in the market for a handful of the stuff for coin counterfeiting or who the hell knows what else. But this... What do you need so much crystal for, if I may ask?"

With a few more sips of liquid confidence in him, Sasha spoke up, "You may not actually. We don't ask how you get it, and you don't ask why we need it. That's how these things work."

Jim stole a quick glance of approval and added, "You heard him."

The gruff man stretched. Jim guessed he'd spent most of his adult life in the crystal mines. Putting a hand up, Joe replied, "Yeah yeah, I know the routine. Okay. Back to business. I'd ask what you're paying, but black is the stuff money is quite literally made of. So, what do you offer in trade?"

Jim nodded at Sasha. *He's on a roll. Might as well let him keep going,* he thought.

Sasha stayed in character as he replied, "My partner and I have a thousand kilos of pushstone. Even trade."

The worker shook his head. "Even trade my ass," he replied with a snort. "You'll have to do better than that. Much better. Pushstone is manufactured by mixing black with water and other common elements. I'd be taking a huge loss." He appeared annoyed. Jim wasn't sure if it was an act or genuine. He glanced at Sasha, but the boy didn't seem to notice.

Sasha's head tilted sideways, "But, pushstone is made from refined black. The process of manufacturing them is quite expensive. We're saving you the work and selling the product to you in its completed state."

The game of trade was underway.

Joe fired the opening shots, "Listen kid, pushstone is just glorified 'crete mixed with black crystal dust. Hardly a rare find. You're basically asking to trade a thousand kilos of pure black crystal for eight hundred kilos of rock and two hundred black. Sweet deal for you. Not me."

Sasha shrugged innocently and replied, "Very well, we can throw in perhaps a hundred kilos of dehydrated cactus fruit." He winced as if reluctant to sweeten the deal.

Joe squinted at Sasha who shrugged and continued, "And of course, a couple hundred kilos of assorted spices from the eastern desert. A rare find."

The tension at the table melted away as Joe chuckled and relaxed back into his seat, "That's better. We got pushstone comin' out our ears here. Spices though. Worth their weight in black when trading with those northern tribesmen loonies."

"It's agreed then," Sasha reached to shake Joe's hand again. Jim smiled inwardly at the flash of pain on the boy's face. To his credit though, he didn't break character.

With their deal concluded, Joe stood up. Dismissing himself, he quickly plodded through the crowd and out the door.

"So," Sasha sipped his beer with his uncrushed hand, "now that that's all done, let's enjoy some music and drinks. Waitress! Another round for my… business partner and myself."

Jim sighed. It was going to be a long, uncomfortable night but, hell, the kid earned it.

Outside the Blue Belly Saloon, at a poorly maintained wooden table, priest Holar nursed a stein of sweetmead. He'd tracked the two men, or rather the man and the boy, to this place hours before. Public places were hardly suitable for the dangerous possibilities that came with confronting a feral Awakened, particularly a Prime of earth.

Holar knew little of this Awakened of earth, but he knew that he must be patient when tracking him, and diplomatic when the time for words inevitably came. The hours he had spent, separated from Jim and Sasha by only a wall of sandstone, had not been wasted.

As the night dragged on, he had sat quietly, 'listening' to the man's every emotion.

It was an oddly intoxicating experience. The longer Holar listened, the more relaxed he somehow felt. It wasn't that his quarry was a particularly tranquil individual. In fact, he sensed mostly apprehension and annoyance from the man. No, it was the act of tapping into his emotions that seemed to relax Holar.

He stored that curiosity away in the back of his mind for later review, because now, the target was leaving. Holar lowered his head and tightened his hood ever so slightly as a man, perhaps in his early thirties, and a teenager emerged from the saloon. They walked briskly downhill in the direction of the docks and were soon swallowed by the darkness of the late night street.

Holar settled his tab with a handful of black coins on the table and began his final pursuit.

It was nearly 4AM as they made their way back to the ship. Even at such an early hour, the city was alive. Life simply migrated from the merchant quarter to back alleys and "watering holes." Saloon music and laughter poured out from a dozen buildings within earshot.

After midnight, the gas fed street lamps were extinguished, but it did little to slow the nightlife. Men and women staggered to and fro with smaller Manza oil lamps, or candles in hand. Some took their chances feeling around in the dark.

Turning down a quiet alleyway, Sasha, a bit tipsy, commented, "Well, that went well enough."

Jim nodded as they plodded on. Their footsteps echoed off the cobblestone road and brick buildings. "The trade or the drinking?" he asked. He grabbed Sasha by the arm to keep him from stumbling. Sasha had held his beer rather well for someone of his size, but Jim had never been much of a drinker. Sure, a little alcohol could be nice every one in a while, but a clear head was one of the few assets he felt he always had.

Sasha laughed and hiccuped, "Oh, I've been meaning to ask you about your… abilities."

Jim's pace didn't slow. As the noise and laughter died, he moved downhill toward the docks with renewed determination. The silence of the resident quarter drew attention to the ringing in his ears. He shook his head and then stumbled. *Perhaps I did have a bit too much,* he thought. "Go ahead and ask, but I'm not sure I'll be much help," he replied.

"What was your awakening like?" Sasha asked, "I mean, I've been told, most people whose awakenings occur during a near death experience almost always die from it. For the few survivors, well the instructors back at the monastery called you… them, ferals."

Jim shrugged, "If by feral you mean, out of control? Yeah, that's about right. Imagine sticking your hand into a fire. The heat is so intense, it goes from burning agony to needle-like pain, then, almost a… cold. That's a bit like how it feels."

When Jim said no more, Sasha said, "They say that your initial awakening is the most powerful you will ever be, that people die from it because it's the absolute limit of your body's abilities. I'm not so sure though. After all, that display back on the ship was pretty impressive."

Jim thought back to their earlier encounter on the Liberator. "I'm not really sure how I did it. My life was in danger and, suddenly, I knew what to do. It's like the sand and rock was speaking to me. Strange, I know."

Sasha chortled, "No, not so strange. It's the same for a fire Awakened. I only had a few months of training, but my instructors at the monastery taught me, controlling your element is like having a conversation. We command it do something, and it does."

"You should have stayed in school, boy. We could have taught you so much more," a strange voice echoed from the darkness.

Acting on instinct, Jim reached to his side for a scimitar that wasn't there. Entering the city required one to surrender any weapons or leave them behind on your ship. Of course, mercenaries and hired thugs always found ways of smuggling gear in, but Jim and Sasha had been in a hurry.

The two turned back to back and scanned the darkness for the source of the voice.

The man spoke again. As he did, his figure emerged from somewhere behind them, his shadow separating from that of a sagging old lamppost. "Calm yourselves," he began. "I intend no harm. Believe me, had I meant to, killing you would have been far too easy." With a twisted grin, he added "Feral or not."

The man stepped fully into the moonlight and removed his hood, revealing the lightly-seamed face of a person in the early days of old age. His hair was white in the pale light but Jim suspected it still had hints of blonde in it. It was his piercing grey eyes, though, that sent a shiver up his spine.

Sasha spoke first, trying his best to sound confident, "What the hell is a priest doing here? You know the law against your type in this place." His quaking voice betrayed him however.

A momentary rage flashed over the man's face but was quickly replaced with practiced calm. "Boy, the law doesn't ban my type. Were that the case, you too would be trespassing. It simply prevents us from involving ourselves in government affairs or establishing a monastery here."

He sighed and added, "I am but an old priest that wishes to talk with fellow Awakened friends. Surely there's no crime in that."

"So talk," Jim said, crossing his arms, "and make it fast. We have places to be." Sasha was shaking next to him. He kept his hands buried deep in his pockets. Fear crept over the boy's face.

What did they do to him in that monastery? Jim wondered.

The priest bowed slightly and said, "My children, you are lost. The Prophetess, blessed be her benevolence, wishes only for your safety, from yourselves as much as others. As an Awakened of air, I sensed your presence within the city and felt it only right to find and help you. If you would return with me to our monastery in Golden Spire, I would be-"

"Monastery my ass!" Sasha exclaimed. "Those places are cages where you brainwash other awakened so they can be controlled." He practically spit the last word out.

The priest shot an annoyed glance at Sasha and asked, "Young man, tell me. Does the bird see his cage as a restriction, or rather as protection from a dangerous world of predators? Surely, when you release him, it's only a matter of time before he's killed by a vicious creature looking for an easy meal. We offer you that same protection. You see, you two are a danger to others, but not nearly as much as they are to you. Where they would use you for your power, we would help you hone those abilities to enrich the world around you."

"And what of the enslavement of your mind? Is that 'freedom' too?" Jim asked.

"What slavery?" the priest replied. "I am in my right mind. I know who I am. My name is Holar Prinn. I was born in the city of Gateway, in the Unaligned League. I have a mother and father, and a history of which I am fully aware. By the way, you may call me Priest Holar, or Holar will do fine as well."

"Right, and tell me, Holar, have you ever had any desire to visit them again, do anything or go anywhere that the Prophetess doesn't tell you to?" Sasha asked.

Holar paused for a moment but quickly recovered. "Why would I?" he replied, his voice elevated. "The Prophetess is everything I need. To serve her is to court bliss."

Jim could sense the man's patience was growing thin. His words were coming quicker and through gritted teeth.

Sasha finally stopped fiddling in his pockets as he spoke again, "I spent a short time courting that 'bliss' you speak of, and you know what I found? Darkness."

From his pockets, Sasha drew a lighter. With one quick motion, he struck the engaging lever. A small flame emerged, but it was all he needed. Sparing no moment, he thrust his open palm toward the priest.

In an instant, the flame jumped from the lighter to form a ball that levitated centimeters from Sasha's hand. Before the priest could react, Sasha willed the ball into a wall of red plasma. The barrier moved quickly, striking the priest before he could react, thrusting him backward into the side of a nearby stone building.

"Run!" Sasha shouted.

The pair sprinted for their lives. As they ran, their steps echoed off the walls around them. Ahead, the coming sun had just begun to transform the eastern sky with deep purples and oranges. Warm colors played upon the stone street beneath their feet, casting long shadows behind them.

The older man must have been in excellent physical condition. From behind, they could hear his pursuing steps as he gained ground quickly. He roared at them. Rounding the last alleyway, they burst onto Main Street.

For a moment, Priest Holar thought he was dreaming. His vision filled with the brilliance of stars, the ones swimming through his head and the ones in the night sky. It took him a moment to recall the wall of flame and the intense heat as it blew him backwards, the sound of rushing wind as he was thrown, and the sickly thud as his head bounced off the stone alley street.

He had been so focused on the Prime of earth, and if he were honest, the strange feeling of calm that the man instilled in him. *I should have been watching the boy,* he groaned inwardly. *She'll no doubt punish me for that.*

It was the second thought which cleared his head and brought him back to his feet. Still fighting back smoke-filled tears and a throbbing at the back of his head, Holar willed himself forward and sprinted.

He'd lost only a few seconds, but it might be enough to ensure his failure. And failure... well, failure existed in the Prophetess' lexicon right next to "termination."

The further they ran, Jim began to hope. Their sloop was in sight. Only a few hundred paces away, the small sail was black against the waking sky. Suddenly, Jim felt a tingling across his body. The hairs stood up on his head and neck. Then, in a flash of white light, arcs of lightning leapt from the street lamps, seeking him out.

Rage coursed through Holar's mind. Using methods taught to him and generations of priests, he replaced all doubt and uncertainty with the rage of his Prophetess. The oneness of purpose that it brought him, the clarity of his hate. These were the things he needed now.

Holar's hands were outstretched as he began to draw on his awakened power. His pace didn't slow, despite so much of his concentration being drawn to the hunt and his gathering inner storm. It was as if the Prophetess quickened his feet so his mind could summon the power he would need.

The crescendo of power within himself was nearing and as it did, steel lamposts lining the street began to glow blue and crackle with electric current. Soon, very soon, he would conclude the hunt.

Stealing a glance backwards, Jim could see the old man in full sprint as if his age were nothing. His arms were outstretched in typical Awakened fashion. From his hands, lightning reached out, clinging to anything metallic: lamps, window frames, sewer covers, doorknobs. All were conduits for his Awakened power.

This would be a great time for those Awakened powers! Jim told himself. He stretched his hand out in the hopes that the motion would somehow activate his abilities. It didn't and they continued to stumble down the steeply-graded street.

Webs of energy crackled and snapped from all sides and the streets were awash in white light. Jim could feel stings of pain as a few of the bolts lashed his back. It would only be a few more seconds before the priest overtook them and he would be roasted, or worse, knocked out and taken to be "re-educated."

Sasha, breathing heavily, started to slow his pace. His pyrotechnic display had instantly drained him. Wrapping one arm under his struggling friend, Jim helped him remain upright as they limped downward.

"You're mine!" The priest shouted as he released the torrent of hatred within himself. Then, he heard the rumbling.

Sasha finally collapsed, giving way to exhaustion. "Just go, Jim," he panted. "At least one of us has to make it back."

"Oh shut up," Jim replied. "If I can just figure out how this damned Awakened power works, I could just..." he held his arms out and imagined the street in front of the priest collapsing inwardly. He willed it. He begged it. He didn't know what the hell he was doing.

But somehow, one of these methods seemed to have an effect. A deep rumbling suddenly echoed off the houses on either side of the street. There was a crash of glass followed by another and another.

"Jim, what did you -"

As soon as he realized what was happening, Holar's concentration broke. He stole a moment of uncontrollable laughter as he watched the street nearly twenty meters ahead of him collapse inward. But, it didn't stop there. A nearby house groaned and cracked as it slumped forward into the growing pit. He could hear the screams of its occupants inside.

"Foolish, feral idiot," Holar laughed, "This is why you should have come quietly." He stretched his arms outward again as he regained control of his emotions.

"You are a danger to everyone else as much as yourself. Now, come with me before more damage is done to these poor people."

"Go to hell," Jim shouted back as his face turned in anguish. The house had now slid fully into the pit and the screams were suddenly silenced. He tried to will the sinking earth underneath the building to push it back up, but instead, it slipped further. He couldn't process what he'd just done, but he had to run, had to help those people… had to…

The priest's silhouette shrugged. Again, the street lit up as the man summoned his vast Awakened energy. Crackling electricity leapt down the sides of the street, using the metal lamp posts as a conduit. Jim considered trying again, but the thought of harming more innocents weighed heavily on him. He threw Sasha over his shoulder and turned to run, for what little good that might do. Holar's attacks were nearly upon them now.

Suddenly, through the white light engulfing them, Jim spotted two quick flashes from the direction of their ship. Two zips past Jim's ear were followed quickly by a *pop pop*. He suddenly remembered, Henry!

The familiar sound of bullets hitting flesh was followed by a grunt. At once, the lightning ceased. Jim looked back to see the body of the priest collapse with a dull *thud*.

Jim took a deep breath. "Can you stand?" he asked Sasha as he set him gently on his feet.

The boy swayed back and forth a few times, but finally steadied himself. "Yeah, I… I think so."

"Good, get back to the ship. I think we need to have a little conversation with priest Holar back on the boat, and I can't carry you both."

The authorities would no doubt be on the way. It was time to get the priest and get out of Rock Bottom.

Chapter IX

The Golden Spire

The *clop clop clop* of Vachir's footsteps echoed off high alabaster walls as he walked double-time through the streets of Golden Spire. Each building slumbered in the rising morning sun, despite it being near nine in the morning. In fact, if he closed his eyes, it would have been as quiet as a stroll through the Mensora Foothills.

As he turned from one tree-lined avenue to a wider and much more worn one, he felt a pang of disgust in his gut. *So much plantlife. So much water needed to sustain it. Such a waste.*

Golden Spire was the capital of the Holy Land, and indeed the only city within its borders. It sat atop a massive source of underground water, which its ruler, the Prophetess, held complete control over. She used it to sate her stagnant population of entirely converted Awakened priests and acolytes, and of course the many trees and decorative bushes dotting nearly every avenue.

Vachir had grown up in the Jindagee swamp town of South Greenlake. But even those lucky enough to live next to the lake knew just how precious of a commodity water was throughout Ruin. Having spent the last two decades in service of the Federation military, he'd spent very little time at home, and most of his time on various desert campaigns against the Alliance.

There was a saying that both sides shared; "Until you have spilled your blood upon the sands, you will never appreciate life giving water."

He turned down 9th Street, which was now shaded by the immense structure of Golden Spire, the building that gave the city its name. The entire city was laid out like a sundial. In mid-summer, the shadow of Golden Spire would fall on each street at exactly the time of day it represented. As he was on 9th Street, and the shadow was directly upon him, it was 9AM. All of the city's streets were arrayed this way to represent Ruin's 25-hour day-cycle.

Suddenly, a whooshing sound followed by a hiss reached his ears. He stopped for a moment and looked up. A large balloon emerged from behind one of the nearer houses. As it floated by overhead, Vachir could make out a few figures wearing the typical blue robes of priests. They were standing like statues at the airship's wooden rails, staring out upon the city.

Somewhere deep in the tower, a clock bell rang out. Though the tower was nearly an hour's brisk walk away, he felt the ringing in his chest.

At once, doors flung open, and thousands of men and women, dressed in blue robes, began to fill the street. It was as if someone had flipped the switch on Golden Spire and spurred its residents to activity.

Nobody even bothered to look at him, and conversation was almost completely absent. Each person proceeded to whatever destination their menial jobs required of them, and they did so blissfully. Each person wore a grin. Or something approximating one. To Vachir, the expression looked like a mix of happiness and horror, and that eerie tension worsened the closer he grew to the Prophetess' chambers deep in the heart of the city.

"General Vachir, enter, now."

The voice of the Prophetess pierced Vachir's skull. The pain of her telepathic summon was dizzying.

Vachir took a moment to center himself before pulling the arm length jeweled handle of the chamber door. It glimmered under the gaslight of nearby wall lanterns. The Prophetess rarely received visitors, but her clockwork and priest servants kept the underground palace immaculate.

Vachir shuddered at what waited on the other side of those great doors.

Suddenly, a complicated collection of cogs and gears came to life behind the cool metal. *CLICK CLICK zzz CLICK.* Somewhere a valve hissed as it brought the complicated mechanism to life. Puffs of steam escaped through age worn cracks in the massive frame as it awoke from its mechanical rest.

With a final *SNAP,* the clockwork door crept open. Cool air sighed out of the chamber beyond. The moistness of it felt foreign upon Vachir's skin. He stood against it feeling sticky and uncomfortable in his FCF uniform.

The meeting hall beyond the door was massive. The room had been built centuries earlier as a giant attunement chamber for the Prophetess to project her Awakened power. She was the only known Awakened of water in the land of Ruin, and by far the most powerful wielder of any element in known history. And then there was her age.

Through powers beyond Vachir's understanding, she appeared to have mastered immortality. Where the average Awakened individual could hope to live a hundred years, and a Prime two or three hundred, she had continued on for nearly a thousand, or such was the rumor: she still looked no older than a woman in her mid-twenties.

The heavy footsteps of his military boots echoed off the smooth stone walls. The domed structure was inlaid with intricate circular patterns of black-crystal. Vachir thought, careful to hide his disgust under layers of mental control, *Probably enough crystal here to pay for the food of a thousand people for a hundred years.*

For centuries, black crystal had been used for currency, airship fuel, and landship pushstones, but it wasn't until the first Awakened were born that its elemental augmentation properties were wholly realized.

To this day, wars were fought for control of precious deposits and mines. More daring wanderers would face fierce beasts and weather in the deep desert in the hopes of making their fortunes. Many had ventured. Few survived. But here, there was plenty.

Throughout the chamber, clockwork manservants darted around, going about their assigned errands as quickly and inconspicuously as possible. Her Grace had a temper and was known to lash out at the nearest unfortunate victim.

Vachir walked across the stone chamber floor, careful to cast his eyes downward. As he neared the throne, he could feel the icy stare of the Prophetess boring into his soul. In the chamber, her powers were greatly amplified by the black crystal inlays. An outburst or stray burning thought would be all she needed to end him.

The walkway to the throne was flanked by two crescent shaped ponds covering much of the massive round chamber. Its design was intended to imitate the eye-shaped flag of the Holy Order when viewed from above.

Vachir kneeled as he reached the lower dais of the platform. "Your Grace, I have located a Prime Awakened of earth. I come bearing this news in the hopes it will help abate my failure in capturing the Lib...uh Dagger.."

The Prophetess spoke, her voice both in his mind and echoing through the chamber. "Rise, general. I don't like talking to the top of your head."

Reluctantly, he fixed his attention on her and was immediately struck by what he saw.

The Prophetess was draped in a flowing robe of reflective blue desert silk. It shimmered in the glow of the chamber pools. Her dress flowed down steps of stone like gently flowing water.

As she descended the steps toward him, he averted his gaze.

She stopped on the final step, standing face-to-face with him, forcing him to look into her eyes. They set his blood to ice in his veins.

She stared at him, into him, probing, digging, questioning. He mustered the entirety of his mental faculties and buried his inner feelings from her ever-perceptive powers.

Even for a being as powerful as she, the age old adage held true, "The eyes are the windows to the soul." Vachir knew, he was looking into the eyes of someone… something ancient. What may have once been a woman centuries ago had been twisted, by the years or experiences, perhaps both. She was little more than a demon in human skin now.

The Prophetess' tone pitched into something between motherly and playful. "Vachir, you're holding something back. You wouldn't be keeping anything from your Prophetess, would you?" She stuck out her lower lip in mocked disappointment.

He had to think of something.

"Your Grace, I'm just… containing my excitement. Finding a Prime of earth was unexpected and invigorating. However, it would be inappropriate to celebrate such a discovery in light of the losses during last week's attack."

The chamber was silent, save for the gentle drip of water. Just as the silence grew uncomfortable, the Prophetess smiled. "Surely. The loss of interceptors and their ether cubes is shameful. Not to mention, expensive." She failed to mention the loss of lives. "A normal man would have been emptied for such a failure."

The Prophetess gently brushed his cheek with her cold hands. He shuddered as his face numbed and his body weakened. Her power to sap others of will and strength was absolute, and Vachir suspected, the secret to her eternal youth.

A glint of twisted pleasure flashed across her eyes as she watched Vachir squirm. Another moment and she withdrew, her point having been made. "However, I share your good spirits. To hear we have finally found a Prime of earth; what luck! Two Primes on the same ship, no less! I think it may finally be time to put my spy to work."

"Are you sure the spy has not been discovered?" Vachir asked.

"When it comes to mind walkers, one can never be entirely certain," the Prophetess admitted. "Their nature is such that they can do little more than influence the one they occupy. Once they emerge, it begins to damage the mind of their host. Most last only a few weeks. Lord Scieth is awaiting a specific instruction from me before the clock starts ticking. Until then, his host is entirely unaware that they are being occupied, aside from the occasional breakthrough of Scieth's... *personality*."

Like the Prophetess, her son the mind walker, Lord Scieth was nearly as cruel. Unlike her, however, he was unable to speak to minds across vast distances, instead having to occupy a victim's mind through direct contact. Once his personality emerged, the victim would die within weeks and the mind walker would move onto their next host, continuing the vicious cycle.

"And if the sabotage fails," Vachir responded slowly, "Lord Scieth would be lost to you." Vachir hid relief within himself at that thought.

The Prophetess thought on his words. A brief flash of genuine worry crossed her face. For a moment, she looked years older. He felt as if these brief moments were all that remained of whoever she had once been.

Then, a familiar storm gathered in her expression. After another moment, she shook her head and grabbed his hands. Squeezing just a little too hard, again, sapping his strength as she replied, "That is why you will not fail. If you do, it will be the last such failure of yours I have to endure."

Her voice was ice again. His dizzying headache returned with a vengeance as he replied shakily, "Yes my Prophetess... ugh... I... will do as you..."

She withdrew her mental probe. Her face was awash with pleasure before she continued, "Of course you will do as I command. You may be a soldier of the Free Citizen's Federation, but don't forget, the leaders of Ruin answer to me. By extension, so do you."

How could he possibly forget? The Warlord's Alliance and Free Citizens of Ruin had been subjugated in the Last Holy War nearly two hundred and fifty years ago now. Her priests polluted every city, town, and village south of The Protectorate with their presence. They were always on the lookout for potential Awakened as well as any seeds of rebellion looking to take root. Agitators were dealt with in a swift and public way.

The last rebellion, known by most as the Second War of the South, had ended in the deaths of hundreds of thousands. However, that conflict had also spawned the thorn in the Prophetess' side that was the crew of the repurposed Dagger class airship.

While the whole of Southern Ruin had cowed to her power, Alia's raiders had continued the fight against the Prophetess, and aboard the Liberator they would emerge from hiding to raid monasteries and empty them of their students before disappearing again into the night sky.

Many times, the Holy Land had dispatched airships to hunt them down, and many times they had failed. Vachir would never admit it aloud, but he coveted the freedom of Alia and her rebels.

"Now, my dear Vachir. I believe business is concluded. On to more... pleasurable matters. Will you please join me in my chamber for a more private conversation?"

As beautiful as she may have appeared on the outside, he dreaded such requests. "I really must return to my soldiers and set the plan in motion. Perhaps we..."

She grabbed him by the elbow and his strength left him. Forced into compliance by her overwhelming power, he could only obey her wishes.

"I'll be gentle."

No, she wouldn't.

Epilogue

"Wake up!"

Holar groaned. He recognized the voice, but he didn't want to open his eyes.

"I said wake up dammit!"

He felt his body shake but still didn't move. He longed only for the warm embrace of sleep.

"Here, let me try," came a voice sounding oddly like a clockwork servant. *But that's impossible. The only clockwork men around were servants of the Prophe-*

CLANG!

The cold metal hand struck Holar awake with one swift strike and sent him sputtering across a wooden floor.

As his senses grudgingly returned, he felt the familiar sway of a landship and heard the gentle flapping of canvas against wind. He could feel the burn of fresh bullet wounds in his right shoulder as well as the flesh of his inner right thigh.

"Where am I? Who" he turned to gaze on a sun darkened face covered in a short cut black beard. It took him a moment to realize… it had been so dark after all. "Ahh the Prime Awakened."

"Look here," Jim said, pointing to the aft of the small landship. "Tell me what you see."

Holar leaned forward to push himself to a standing position, but he fell on his face, suddenly realizing that his hands were tied behind his back. He heard a metallic chuckle. Then, the same cold metal hands he'd felt a moment earlier grabbed him by the collar and lifted him to a standing position. The abrupt effortless movement nearly sent him falling forward again, but he was steadied by an unshakable grip.

"He asked you a question," came the tin voice.

In the distance, a familiar city bathed in the first morning light was shrinking away.

"I see Rock Bottom," he replied.

"That's right," Jim said. "Rock Bottom, the only city within hundreds of kilometers, and we are sailing away from it at present. The further we go, the less chance you have of returning to it alive. Answer my questions quickly and we will drop you in the sand to make your way back. Take too long and we will still drop you, but you will be that much further away. I doubt you'll survive the walk back. These dunes are crawling with cannibals."

"Well," came the clockwork man's reply with a chuckle, "perhaps not so many as a few days a-."

"Not now, Henry," Jim interrupted.

"Very well, ask your questions," Holar replied, "though it's all pointless." As his mind was clearing, so too was his confidence. Though it somehow felt empty. This man, this 'Jim' seemed to dampen the Prophetess' pull on his mind just by his very presence. Part of him reveled in the peace it brought, but another part fought against its novel influence.

"How long have you been pursuing us?" Jim asked.

"Since you were born," Holar replied with a shrug and a grin. "The Prophetess calls to us all, and we all return to her eventu-"

CLANG! Holar's head rolled against another blow.

"No stupid answers," Henry shouted. "If we wanted a reading of your *sacred* texts, then we would take one out of our kindling supplies. They do burn so *easily*."

That should have enraged Holar, but he felt nothing. *Curse this Awakened of earth. He muddles my mind. She should have sent more than a single priest to apprehend him. I must get out of this place.* He realized that his last thought had been, at least in part, a criticism of the Prophetess, and it frightened him. Again, he tried to summon her anger to suppress the earth Awakened's influence.

Finally, he said, "I smelled your unique gifts when you neared the city."

There was a moment of quiet broken only by the rising gusts of the twilight winds.

Jim stared into the priest's eyes, judging the truth of his statement. "Fine," he suddenly replied. "Next question. How do I keep from being... smelled by your kind again?"

At that, Holar laughed. "You can't hide yourself from me, from her. You are known to us no matter where -"

CLANG!

"OW!"

"Less bravado please," Henry suggested. "Thank you."

The priest stared daggers at the man and machine. "Tell me, what happened to the poor souls in that house you buried? Were you under the guidance of my queen, such a mistake would never have-"

CLANG!

"Questions are off limits too," Henry said, this time hitting Holar a second time to drive the point home.

Henry's strikes were beginning to resolve Holar's dazed mind as his rage welled up. He couldn't use his powers, but he still had the power of his tongue.

"You fools!" he seethed. "You defy the Prophetess with your very existence. Were it up to me, I would kill you all for you insulance, but I serve one far greater than myself. She has deemed you worthy of reclamation, well, *you* at least." he said sneering at Jim. "As for you," he continued, turning to Henry, "She would just as soon turn your *traitorous* chassis into scrap, and use your ether cube to-"

Henry interrupted him. "I'll just stop you there."

CLANG!

"Uggggh!" Holar screamed. "I will destroy you! We will cleanse the world of your kind. You can not hide from us. Nowhere escapes her-"

"Bye then!"

Holar suddenly found himself sailing through the air, coming up very quickly on a sand dune ahead. This was going to hurt.

"Sorry Jim," Henry said with the clockwork equivalent of a grin. He brushed his metallic hands off. "I don't think dear mister Holar was going to be much help. Like all priests, he's more or less a walking religious text. Void of individual thought."

Jim nodded. "Seems so. He was right about those people though."

Henry was slow to speak this time. "We… we don't know that they are dead."

"And we never will since we left in such a hurry. I'm a murderer, Henry. There's no way around that."

Henry paused again as he considered his words carefully. Finally, he said, "Yes, if you did kill them, you will have to live with that mistake for the rest of your life. I realize that isn't the most comforting answer, but I think what you need now is to accept what happened and work toward never making such an error again."

Jim deflated.

"The priest was right about one thing," Henry said, trying to turn the conversation.

"What's that?" Jim asked.

"Your power is untamed. But, that's why you should be grateful."

"Grateful… why?" Jim asked.

"Because," Henry replied, "the Liberator is filled with others like you. Others who can teach you how to hone this gift of yours, who can understand what your struggles are. I realize we are strangers to you, but the crew is, well, they are good people. Take Sasha for instance," he pointed to the hatch leading below deck. "He's only been with us a short while, but he's family. Sure the captain had to treat him to a bit of tough love, but he accepted it, learned from it, and has grown from it. You can do the same."

Jim nodded but said nothing. For a while, they both stared quietly at the horizon.

Jim finally broke the silence, "Hey, I have a question."

"Sure," Henry replied. His hue of blue brightened. "I'm always eager for stimulating conversation. More so after being stuck on this barge while you two had all the fun in the city."

"Are all priests as… single-minded as that one?"

Henry laughed. "Actually, that one was nearly coherent compared to most I've seen. Did you see the way he kept looking at you?"

"No," Jim replied.

"I've never been accused of being a keen or quiet observer of behavior, but even I could see, he was fascinated, and perhaps a bit frightened by you."

"To be honest, neither of those sound very good," Jim replied. He leaned over the railing and watched as the clock tower of Rock Bottom dissolved into the heat of the morning.

Henry came over to join him and set his metal hand on Jim's shoulder. "One thing is clear," he said. "If the prophetess didn't know about you before, she sure does now. I think it might have been a bad idea to let that priest live."

"Perhaps," Jim sighed. "Perhaps."

So close now, so close. I heard your call, mother. Soon, you will hear my voice again. Soon, the Liberator will light up the night sky and the ashes of those who refused you will fertilize the hillside.

I must only wait now for the right moment.

So close now. The plan is in motion.

End of Volume I

Want more Ruin? Then head on over to *www.authocracy.com/sign-up* for access to exclusive fact-files, data entries and more.

And be sure to follow us on social media to keep up-to-date with future projects and all things Authocracy.

Facebook: @AuthocracyStudios
Twitter: @real_authocracy
Instagram: @authocracy_studios
Website: www.authocracy.com

Thank you for supporting independent publishing!

Authocracy
Publishing